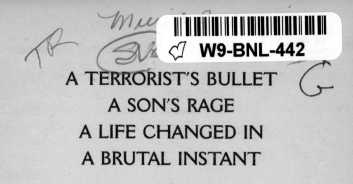

A TERRORIST'S BULLET
A SON'S RAGE
A LIFE CHANGED IN
A BRUTAL INSTANT

◆

The door burst open. Connor McGuire's son felt his breath catch in his throat as three masked men rushed in, all brandishing weapons. Two of the men took aim at Frankie, his mother, and sister while the third strode to the table. A surprised and enraged Connor McGuire began to rise and turn. The move brought him eye to eye with the muzzle of an automatic pistol. It was aimed point-blank at his face. And just as suddenly as Frankie's da saw it, the gun jumped with a roar, like a clap of thunder. The back of Connor McGuire's skull came off and for Frankie McGuire, directly in its path, the world turned a hot, sticky red. . . .

THE DEVIL'S OWN

a novel by
Christopher Newman

based on a story by
Kevin Jarre
screenplay by
David Aaron Cohen &
Vincent Patrick and
Kevin Jarre

A DELL BOOK

Published by
Dell Publishing
a division of
Bantam Doubleday Dell Publishing Group, Inc.
1540 Broadway
New York, New York 10036

ISBN: 0-440-22387-3

Printed in the United States of America

Published simultaneously in Canada

April 1997

10 9 8 7 6 5 4 3 2 1

OPM

this one is for Evelyn

THE
DEVIL'S
OWN

———————◆———————

PROLOGUE

━━━━━ ◆ ━━━━━

North Channel of the Irish Sea
off Carnlough

Northern Ireland, 1973

On this rare, crystal-clear day, young Frankie
McGuire knew the contentment that any master of his own universe knows. The breeze-rippled
sea was that same deep, unfathomable blue as Connie Murphy's eyes, and for the second time in his
young life he'd been allowed by his father to take
the helm of the family fishing boat. That was over
two hours ago, after a shared midday meal of mack-
erel and sharp cheese on hearth-baked brown bread.
Frankie still had the wheel under his da's calm but
watchful eye.

"Comin' up on them dangerous shoal rocks off
Cushendall, lad," his father murmured. "'T' port a

bit more, son. Easy. There you have it. Very nicely done."

Frankie felt his chest swell and wished Connie Murphy could see him now. Indeed, he spent the idle hours of each and every day dreaming of how he would some day own his own deep-sea fishing boat. He would work these same beloved waters while pretty Connie tended home and hearth. They would live a life together like his father and mother shared, without the noisy presence of his sister to dampen their bliss. Ah, how young Frankie Mc-Guire yearned for that day. He would hold his true love's hand all through the night, and kiss her as often as he wished.

After listening to the weather report, Frankie's da had spun the onboard radio dial in search of a news broadcast from Belfast, forty miles to the south. Frankie already knew plenty about the *troubles*. They had set men like Connie's da and his own father at odds. And lately, those troubles had intensified. As much as he loved the infant Jesus and the Virgin, he could not fathom why a family's place of worship could make all that much difference. Didn't he and Connie share the same bright ginger hair, the same mischievous blue eyes and pale, freckled flesh that burned such an angry red in the summer sun?

". . . say clashes escalated between Catholic residents along the Falls Road and the army after a rubber bullet killed a seven-year-old girl," the announcer droned. "It was fired by a British soldier to disperse a Catholic protest march, which threatened to escalate toward violence."

"Bollocks!" Frankie's da snarled. He reached to switch the radio off in disgust. "It has escalated to violence now, you bleeding buggers. Damn you all to the deepest hole in hell."

The fact that it was a seven-year-old girl who had been killed, precisely the same age as Connie, struck Frankie with a strange, unknowing fear. Why, he wondered? What possible threat could a girl like Connie pose to any grown man, let alone to a soldier? He looked up toward his father, his fingers still gripping the spokes of the wheel.

His father read the bewildered look in Frankie's eyes and clapped one of those callused and weather-beaten fisherman's hands on Frankie's shoulder. "Don't ask me why, lad. It's a question I can't answer. They just are what they are."

Frankie's eyes had returned to the sea. Half a mile to the leeward, the cliffs below Cushendall reflected bright in the afternoon sunlight. "What are, Da?"

"The big boys rule."

Puzzled, Frankie glanced up at his father once again.

"You pick up a gun," his father explained, "someone gets a bullet."

Father and son trudged home a half hour later than usual that evening, the summer sun still hours from setting at fifty-five degrees latitude. Both could feel the rumbling of hunger in their bellies, but neither paid it much mind. They would have their suppers soon enough, and each was content within his own parameters. Theirs was a day's work well done. Six miles north of the Scottish isle of Islay in the open Atlantic, they'd met an Estonian trawler's tender craft. Frankie's father had shown a heavyset man in a grease-stained sweater a piece of paper. In exchange, he had taken one hundred kilos of fresh-caught salmon into the ice-packed hold of his boat, along with a pair of bulky parcels sewn into paraffin-impregnated canvas. It was the third time that summer that such a meet had occurred. Frankie had been told on the first occasion to keep his mouth shut, to say nothing to his chums about it. That was the first time his da had ever let him steer the boat. On the day of the second such meeting, the weather had been stormy and Frankie spent most of the voyage puking his breakfast of oatmeal and bacon over the side.

"I don't think I'll be stopping at the pub for a pint t'night, lad," his da declared as they reached the fork in the road. "Your mother will be worried, us bein' late and all. Maybe later, once chores are done. Y' did well t'day, lad. Your father is proud o' you. You'll make a right fine fisherman yet."

They had gotten underway at dawn and Frankie was tired, but still he puffed his chest with pride. His da was a man other men in Carnlough looked up to. Catholic men, at any rate. When he spoke his mind before the peat fire at Feeney's pub, his rumbling voice filled the low-ceilinged room and the other drinkers were respectful. Connie Murphy said once, earlier that summer, that her father and others thought his da was a troublemaker, but Frankie could not see how. Connor McGuire was fearless, yes. Frankie had never seen him back down to any man, regardless of size. But not a troublemaker. Nay. Connie's own banker father was a troublemaker, always at the head of the parade of Orangemen on Guy Fawkes Day. Frankie's da called it picking the scab of Catholic failure, and roundly cursed Mr. Kelley Murphy for it.

The table looked as though it had been laid for quite some while when the two McGuire men entered their home. Frankie's thirteen-year-old sister, Mary Claire, sat scowling over her lacework in a corner and hardly looked up.

"Ma," she bawled out. "Da's here at last."

Frankie's mother, clearly fraught with nerves, darted into the room tying her apron. She bussed the cheek of her husband in passing and ordered Frankie to wash.

"Move, girl," she ordered Mary Claire. "The fishing went well?" she asked Da.

"Over two hundred pounds of prime salmon, though that bleeding scum Barstow would pay no more than half the going rate for it. Sod the bastard. One day, he'll get his."

With a warm bowl in her hands from the hearth, Frankie's mother stopped and frowned. "Not in front of the children, Connor. Please. It's bad enough, what they hear on the street, without them hearin' it here in their own home, too."

Frankie's da grumbled something under his breath as he moved to stand beside his son at the washbasin.

Once grace was said and Connor McGuire had mashed together equal shares of boiled beef and spuds on his plate, he took a mouthful and surveyed his little family with satisfaction. "Frankie's going to make a right fine fisherman, he will," he announced. "Got an instinctive feel for the helm."

"His marks in school are excellent," Frankie's mother countered. "Father Dunleavy tells me he'll recommend him for a place at the seminary in another two years' time. We could never afford to give him such a fine education as that, Connor."

It was clear from the expression on Connor McGuire's face what he meant to reply to such a notion, but before he could open his mouth, the door behind him burst open. Connor's terrified son felt his breath catch in his throat as three masked men rushed in, all brandishing weapons. Two of the men took aim at Frankie, his mother, and sister, while the third strode toward the table. A surprised and enraged Connor McGuire began to rise and turn. The move brought him eye-to-eye with the muzzle of an automatic pistol. It was aimed point-blank at his face. And just as suddenly as Frankie's da saw it, the gun jumped with a roar, like a clap of thunder. The back of Connor McGuire's skull came off and for Frankie McGuire, directly in its path, the world turned a hot, sticky red.

1

◆

Belfast
Twenty-Four Years Later

The briefing room at SAS clandestine operations headquarters near the River Lagan shipyards was stifling. It was an unusually warm August
that Northern Ireland was experiencing. Harry Sloan
of Her Majesty's Secret Service branch MI5 stood
with his tie loosened and collar unbuttoned before
two squads of SAS wet-work specialists—commandoes trained in the delicate and often brutal art
of clandestine urban guerrilla warfare. The room
was darkened, blackout curtains drawn, and a pathetic oscillating fan set atop the table at his right
hip barely stirred the close, sweat-heavy air. Each
and every one of those ruthlessly schooled killing
machines seated before him was dressed in coveralls
splashed in the muted hues of redbrick dust and concrete. Not a one of them so much as twitched in

betrayal of the slightest discomfort. They were cool in their minds. In their world, that was the only cool that mattered. Harry Sloan knew the feeling. In a time that seemed an eternity ago now, he, too, had been one of the SAS elite. But theirs was a game for much younger men. A fifty-year-old MI5 strategist, Harry embodied a different sort of cool than they. He'd gone to the mat with the best of the bad and survived. Today he got to rest on his laurels.

"This is your target, gentlemen."

The image on the projection screen behind him shifted abruptly with the slide change, now showing the grainy photo of a man caught in three-quarters view by a telephoto lens. He had a scruffy beard, his strawberry-blond hair worn tied back in a little ponytail. His intent blue eyes were focused on some unseen object off camera.

"Frankie McGuire," Sloan continued. "Also known among his comrades and to the tabloid press as Frankie the Angel. Commander, Falls Road Active Service Unit, Belfast Brigade. Known to be responsible for the deaths of eleven regular army, seven RUC officers, and an unknown number of loyalist paras."

Sloan paused to let that sink in, surveying the expressionless faces before him. He might as well have told this lot that McGuire rescued abandoned kittens for all the rise it had gotten out of them. "Bastard has never seen the inside of a cell, which is remarkable, considering the long term of his notoriety. But two days ago we got a break. A Provo bomb maker turned informant has given us a time and location where we can expect Frankie the Angel to put in an appearance. This evening, at eighteen hundred hours."

Another slide change. A burnt-out street in the Beechmount section of Belfast appeared. The pavement was strewn with rubble and parked with battered old cars. "O'Shaughnessey Street, gentlemen. Your target building is the one in the middle of the screen." He indicated a building half boarded up, in better repair than most, with an overgrown empty lot alongside. "Identified as being the Falls Road Unit's latest Belfast safe house. Good location for them, buried deep in a one hundred percent sympathizer-occupied neighborhood. I will now let Brigadier Morris proceed with your briefing, but only after saying that if McGuire is in that building," Sloan nodded at the screen, "I and eleven dead British Army soldiers want very much for you to fetch his arse out of there."

A commando in the front row raised his hand. The movement was as fluid and pretty as a ballet dancer's. "Sir?"

"Yes," Harry acknowledged the broad-shouldered boy.

"Are you very much concerned if he's delivered dead or alive, sir?"

Harry had already begun to move away from that table to make room for the brigadier. He smiled. "From an intelligence perspective, I'm sure you can understand the value of a man like Frankie Mc-

Guire, delivered to us alive. But if dead is the only way he'll come along, then so be it. England will have one less terrorist to worry about."

Over the eleven years since his seventeenth birthday, when he detonated his first bomb in a smoke shop in Donegall Place, Frankie McGuire had, by necessity, become a creature of the Belfast night. Today, he was one of the most hunted men in the so-called United Kingdom, with the blood of at least fifty of the enemy on his hands. There was an Ulster Volunteer Force reward of fifty thousand British pounds on his head. On this particular Wednesday, developments of the past few days demanded that the command structures of the Falls Road Unit and Ballymacarret Unit meet to discuss a security leak. One or the other of them had sprung it inside their ranks, and it needed to be plugged. Quickly. The time settled on was half past six P.M., in the middle of the dinner hour for most citizens and soldiers. Frankie was angry that it couldn't be later, under cover of night, but there were conflicts that others had.

A ragtag group of boys had piled junk in the street to demark goals, and a spirited game of soccer was underway as Frankie slid ghostlike up the block toward his destination. His fingers were so accustomed to the checkered plastic grip of the Glock automatic in his field jacket pocket that it had begun to seem like an extension of his being. A shout startled him as he cut quickly from curb to street to cross, and he glanced up to see a soccer ball hurtle toward him. With a quick sideways head snap, he butted it back toward the field of play without breaking stride. At a low wall beyond the opposite curb, he planted his free hand to vault into the empty lot alongside the safe house. His heart still raced from the surprise of the soccer ball, but no observer, not even an intent one, would have noticed the slightest betrayal of his discomfort. Frankie "The Angel" McGuire had learned long ago to internalize everything: his rage, his pain, any humor he had left, any capacity he had to feel anything, but hate.

When that soccer ball came Frankie's way again to bounce over the wall and into the weeds, an internal antenna went up. He slowed his pace to veer into the lot and retrieve the ball as a scruffy boy with lank, greasy dark hair rushed over from the game.

"Fookin' Brit bugger. Field glasses. Ford parked on the right, end of the street," he gasped, out of breath.

Frankie smiled and tossed the ball back. "Thank y', little brother. In five or ten minutes' time, y' might want to move your game."

SAS Commando Sergeant Nigel Wilson watched the ball go into that lot. The suspicious fellow with the furtive movements flipped it back to the street punk. Their exchange looked cordial enough, but who knew? He raised his two-way to his lips and thumbed the transmit button.

"Hound One to Huntmaster. Could have been the

fox I just saw, headed for the hole. Observed brief exchange. Him and young boy, on the street. Over."

The spooky-smooth voice of the MI5 man came back at him. "Hold your position, Hound One. Half your kennelmates should be in view now. Rover sedan. To the south, coming toward you off Falls Road."

Once inside the O'Shaughnessey Street safe house, Frankie McGuire was suddenly all command. Of the three men with automatic weapons who greeted him on arrival, two were from his own unit and the third was part of the Ballymacarret lot. Good, dependable lads, all.

"Where's Sean?" he demanded of his ranking sentry.

"One floor up. With Dessie."

Frankie turned to the other of his two men. "Get him down here. We've got Brits. Timmy and you, come with me." He patted the back of the Ballymacarret Unit lad to encourage him along, and hurried to an opening created between planks over one streetside window. His arrival there coincided with the appearance of a gray Rover 3000 sedan at the south end of the street. Only a driver was visible in it now, but Frankie knew all their tricks.

Behind McGuire, Sean Geary rushed into the charred, litter-strewn room, a tire iron in one hand and a machine pistol in the other. "Lookout on the roof spotted an armored personnel carrier, Frankie. Way over toward Grosvenor Road, but headed this direction."

Frankie absorbed this news without any appearance of concern. "Flat fix ruse ready?"

"As it'll ever be," Geary replied.

"Go," Frankie ordered. "You two, come with me."

From his command post on Grosvenor Road at the north end of the Beechmount Catholic ghetto, Harry Sloan could literally feel the hatred beamed at him from behind drawn curtains as he raised his radio to his lips. "Keep talking, Hound One. Tell me what you see."

"Lads playing football just called their game off. Don't like the feel of that, sir. Some stupid berk with a spare tire just rolled it past, headed down the street." There was dead air, then: "Damn my eyes. I see the same bastard just went into the house a few minutes ago, sir. And now that I can see the face on him, I'll bet my granny's gold teeth it's Frankie the Angel."

Sloan felt his pulse quicken. Behind him, a tank rumbled up the road. He had to plug one ear to still hear Sergeant Wilson. "Doing what?" he demanded.

"Just standin' there, starin' directly my way, sir. Damnedest thing. It's like he's taunting me."

"Hound Two, Hound Three. Don't wait. Go now," Sloan ordered. Good Christ, what the hell was this, he wondered? Surely not the intended element of surprise.

*   *   *

Two cars back of where that Rover 3000 had parked, Sean Geary rolled the spare tire up over the curb, now with the bulk of an old Hillman Minx between him and his target. As he knelt to feign loosening lug nuts on a flat, he eased the Intratec machine pistol from beneath his oversize shirt and set it in the gutter, within easy reach. Up the block, Frankie emerged from the front door of the safe house to stand staring at the one Brit in the Ford, and then at the other in the Rover. A second Ford Grenada appeared from around the corner at the north end of O'Shaughnessey Street.

"Time to dance," Sean muttered to himself. A smallish man who'd forever been a bundle of hot-wired, high-voltage energy, he could feel the amperage intensify now to heighten his every animal sense.

Frankie, one moment lounging lazily against the front of the house, straightened suddenly to flip his half-smoked cigarette into the street, then bolted toward the low wall and into the empty lot next door from the street. Sean watched the move work like a trigger. Three more heads popped into view inside the target Rover and doors flew open, the occupants surging forth to launch their attack.

One of those British lads was too quick for Sean. Surely not regular Brit army, these fellows. He was at that wall and halfway over it before Geary could snatch up his weapon and draw bead. A second man, Sean just plain missed as he leapt to his feet to spray the street. The remaining two, caught in the open at a dead run, jerked with the impact of his slugs as if they'd been stung by angry hornets. Then they went down in heaps.

Sean bolted back across the street toward another burned-out house, springing the spent clip as he ran. He dropped it, slapping a fresh one into his weapon. By that time, the Brit lookout was half out of his car, yelling at four more commandoes in camouflage, sprinting toward him from the north end of the street. There'd been a security leak somewhere, all right. And if Sean survived this little ordeal, he swore that he and Frankie would root the traitorous bastard out and string him up by his bollocks.

Frankie McGuire had no idea how many of them the Brit Army would send on an op like this, but he had to imagine they had plenty of firepower in reserve. The whole thing had the stink of an inside leak, and that made him even more furious than he was with the Brits. His blood suddenly pumped cold in his veins. He stopped once he gained the temporary sanctuary of the safe house, rather than run deeper to safety. Outside, when that burst of weapons fire died away, he could hear shouts and running footfalls. Experience told him that at least one of the four from that first car had reached the house. Those were the odds. He slipped back into deep shadow and forced himself to wait and listen. There were footfalls down the side of the house, toward the window he'd used as an entrance. But one man was not likely to come in after him alone. There'd be another, and they would time it for the quick kill. A pincer movement, the first two of them.

An instant later, the room exploded with daylight as the makeshift front door caved in. A body hurtled in behind it, and at the same time, a shadowy mass leapt in through the open side window. Both commandoes had planned it to land back-to-back, enabling them to lay down a withering circle of fire in all directions, and not kill each other. Frankie anticipated exactly that, and before they could regain their balance and fire, he shot them both dead. One slug apiece. Each in the head.

Terrence "Dessie" Desmond was too astonished by the size of the gaping hole torn in his right side to fully comprehend what had happened to him. At least not at first. He'd been manning his rooftop lookout post when all the shooting had started below. Determined to hang in there and not leap to the house next door until the last possible moment, he'd hunkered down, prepared to fire on any Brit Army choppers that attempted to land troops in his sector. Then, two floors below, he'd heard the loud snap of an incendiary booby trap, and then screams. It was probably rigged on the stairs, a Sean Geary specialty, and it made Dessie grin to think of some Brit scum snagging it and getting his jewels cooked off. Sadly, he hadn't had long to savor that thought. One instant he hugged shadow in relative tranquility, and the next, the roof door had flown open. Two Brit commandoes in camouflage erupted from the stairwell, one fast on the other's heels. Dessie barely had time to recapture his stolen breath and open fire before they did. He'd managed to get both of them, but one of them got lucky, dirty sod. Those two now lay in a heap, just a few yards distant, but as far as Dessie Desmond was concerned, they may as well have been a thousand miles away. A bullet had torn through his right side, just below the rib cage, and nicked his spine. He watched the life quickly leak out of him and tried to wiggle his toes. He couldn't feel them. Nor could he feel his legs.

Dessie wondered if he'd lost consciousness for a moment. He had no recollection of Frankie Mc-Guire's approach, yet opened his eyes to see his unit commander squatted down on his heels alongside him.

"We've only won here for the moment, Dessie lad," Frankie crooned. He tried to lift him. "Got to go, Dessie boyo."

"Get off wit' y', Frankie McGuire," Desmond whispered. "I'm fookin' done. Go. Save yerself."

Without legs, Dessie was an impossible burden for a man of Frankie McGuire's slender build, despite his astonishing strength. He made another attempt to lift his fallen comrade, and Dessie placed a gentle hand on his arm. "Tanks, Frankie. Listen. Any sec, now, they'll be swarmin' the place. Go."

Left alone at last to make his peace with his God, Dessie Desmond stared skyward to watch the long evening light paint soft strokes of pink around the western edges of the clouds. He'd always loved the quality of this light, the way it made everything man and nature had wrought stand starkly outlined and honest in its place.

Footfalls made the rooftop vibrate as some unseen soul approached. Dessie heard low, muffled voices in conversation. Those footsteps stopped for the duration, then started toward him again once conversation ceased. Dessie's vision had begun to blur and the face of the man who bent down to confront him from above was all soft, indistinct smudges. Still, that voice with its clipped intonations of the British educated class, came through to him with chilling clarity.

"There's still time to save you, lad. I've seen more dead than the devil himself. By my judgment, you're still a long way from his door."

Dessie closed his eyes and tried to block out that voice. The bastards didn't have it in them to let his kind live in peace. Nor did they have the decency to let him die that way, either.

"Listen to me, lad. There's an ambulance on the street below. Hospital isn't five minutes distant. All you need to do to save yourself is give me Frankie McGuire."

Dessie opened his mouth to reply, and the best he could manage was a dry, hoarse whisper. "Up your fucking arse." To punctuate it, he spat blood and saliva in the looming, blurry face.

Expressionless, Harry Sloan rose to his feet and removed a neatly folded white handkerchief from an inside pocket of his suit coat. Slowly, he wiped his face. Staring out over the rooftops of this godforsaken Beechmount ghetto, he sighed, clucked his tongue, and removed a Bren Ten 10 mm automatic from his shoulder rig. Thumb on the hammer, he eased it back, took aim at Dessie Desmond, and pulled the trigger. Across the roof, a uniformed British Army captain rushed from the stairwell, weapon drawn, to see Harry Sloan walking slowly toward him.

Sloan shrugged. "Tried to escape," he explained.

2

Hillsborough, County Down
Northern Ireland, later that week . . .

For three days that seemed like an eternity, Frankie McGuire had lain hidden in a crude crawl space beneath the floor in an empty cottage. Over that span of time, the Irish weather outside had turned thirty degrees colder. Any heat trapped inside the cottage during the warm spell had long since been sucked away. The crawl space was cold and damp, the kind of damp that seeps deep into a man's bones, and Frankie was nearly as cold as he was hungry. The last of the food they'd left for him was gone early that morning. One tin of sardines and a crust of bread wasn't enough to sustain a man who'd burned as many calories as he had, shivering to stay warm.

Each waking moment of that eternity, Frankie had forced his mind back over the days and weeks preceding that Brit commando attack on the O'Shaughnessey Street safe house. He made lists: of who had knowledge of the safe house location, who had known on the Falls Road Unit side about the meeting Wednesday night, and who on the Ballymacarret side was suspect enough to have turned. And the more he racked his brain, the more convinced he became that the source of this treachery was somewhere outside his own unit. He knew all of his people too well. Wednesday evening, three of them had given their lives for the cause. It was someone else, outside his own crowd, and every fine-tuned gut instinct he'd developed over the past fifteen years told him that was a fact.

Outside the cottage, the still of the night was broken by the crunch of car tires on gravel. Through cracks in the floorboards overhead, Frankie saw headlights illuminate the cottage interior for an instant before they were switched off. Then the car engine died, a door whumped softly, and a key was inserted and turned in the door latch. Even the softest footsteps overhead sounded like brush strokes on the head of a snare drum. As they approached where he lay, Frankie scooted as far to one corner of the crawl space as he could squeeze himself, and held his Glock automatic at the ready. It wasn't until he heard the quick knocks and a fist thump on the boards above that he realized he'd been holding his breath.

"Can't a man get any sleep around here?" he growled.

The man who crouched to help lift the floorboards aside was Martin McDuff, a squat, astonish-
ingly strong bullmastiff of a fellow who hailed from
Derry Town. Situated far up the clandestine command chain of the Provisional IRA, he'd been a unit
commander when Frankie first arrived in Belfast. It
was Martin who had seen a keen intelligence buried
beneath all that pent-up rage in the young McGuire,
bent on avenging the murder of his da. Martin had
taken pains to mold it into a controlled rage. He
took a renegade, and bullied him into becoming a
soldier. Then he crafted that soldier into a leader.

"How you making it here, lad?" McDuff asked
softly.

"I'm not. But those sheep in the pasture next door
are beginnin' t' have their appeal. You've brought
food, I hope. I'm ready to eat my shoes."

McDuff unslung a knapsack from across his
broad shoulders and handed it across. Frankie, now
hoisted out of his confinement to sit on the edge of
that open access hole, pawed at the zipper like a
ravenous animal. Inside the sack he found sandwiches wrapped in paper, and several bottled beers.
Before he pried the cap off a bottle to drink, he took
one wolfish bite of boiled ham and cheese on brown
bread.

"There was big turnouts for both Dessie's and
Bernadette's funerals this morning," McDuff reported while Frankie ate. "Fookin' Brit scum lost
eight in that little skirmish and tensions is runnin'
pretty high. T' that crowd, you're the fookin' devil,
Frankie, lad. It's lucky we got y' t' ground."

Frankie grinned as he swallowed his mouthful, and shook his head. "I might not be the devil himself, Martin. But so far as they're concerned? I'm happy t' be the devil's own."

"Aye. Fookin' bastards. Whitehall and MI6 talk peace out o' one side of their mouths, and at the same time have the SAS waiting in the wings t' wipe us out."

"They've never wanted peace," Frankie replied. He pried the cap off a beer and took a long pull. His mouth wiped on his sleeve, he shook his head. "They either want surrender, or t' see us all dead. Me? I'll see them in hell."

"And meanwhile, we've got t' figure out what t' do wit you," McDuff mused.

From off to the north, in the direction of the city, they heard the distant concussive whomp of a military helicopter's rotors. Ears pricked up.

"Coming this way," Frankie observed. "Y' parked your motor out o' sight, I hope."

"In the shearing shed." Martin continued to listen hard to the gunship as it approached. "These routine night patrols are a bloody fookin' nuisance, Frankie lad. We better get out o' sight of the windows. Sounds like he's flyin' straight down our throats."

Together, they scooted to one side of the big, empty room and hugged a wall as the searchlight of the gunship tore the darkness to shreds. For a moment, it seemed to slow as it overflew the cottage. The racket of its rotors and turbine engines was deafening as it shook the window glass.

"Fookin' things," Martin snarled as it finally passed.

Frankie was thoughtful. "What if we had the capacity t' take them down, Martin. Do y' think they'd listen to us then?"

3

◆

Customs and Immigration
Newark International Airport,
two months later . . .

It was a circuitous route which had taken the Falls
Road Unit Commander to the United States of
America. He had embarked on the first leg of that
journey, to the port city of Oran, Algeria, as Francis
Xavier McGuire, fugitive IRA killer. Today, nine
weeks down that twisting road, he approached the
passport station washed clean, as Rory Aloysius Devaney. Along the way he'd taken a three-day rail
trip to the Libyan border and spent two weeks in a
tent dodging spy satellites in the Libyan desert.
He'd flown from there to Sarajevo via Tiranë, Alba-
nia, and then spent a month in Frankfurt, before flying here. Rory Devaney wore his hair cut in a
conservative, businesslike fashion that Frankie Mc-

Guire would never have worn. Nor would Frankie have donned such conservative attire, but then Frankie wasn't Frankie anymore. Rory Devaney wore sensible brogues, chinos and rugby shirts. A sport. A regular all-American wanna-be.

The passport he presented to the Immigration Control officer was issued by the Republic of Ireland, not the Belfast Ulster government. It stated that he was from Ravensdale in County Louth, not far from the border, which would explain his accent. His occupation was listed as motorcycle salesman, and in Germany he'd even been provided with a forged letter of introduction from the director of marketing, Bavarian MotorWerks, motorcycle division.

"How long do you intend to stay, sir?" the officer asked casually. His entry stamp poised, it was clear to Rory that he was satisfied with what he saw, and was only going through the motions.

"I doubt it will go the entire ninety days," Devaney replied. "I've got meetings with the Harley-Davidson factory fellas in Indiana, and then more plans t' visit the better run dealerships here and in Florida. California, too, if time and the budget allow." He smiled and shrugged. "My bosses run a tight ship. I'm accountable for every shilling I spend."

The stamp came down and the passport came back with a curt, friendly-enough nod. "Enjoy your stay, sir."

Rory had been told to look for a burgundy Lincoln Town car once he emerged from the arrivals building. He didn't have to look hard, but was still so unaccustomed to moving freely in the bright light of day that he made his approach cautiously. It was supposed to be an older fellow who would be his contact here. Big, from the description, with a distinguished shock of white hair and a bearing of genteel authority.

Just such a fellow loitered, leaning against one fender of the Lincoln, dressed a bit loudly in kelly-green slacks and a bright yellow cardigan. It looked as though he'd just come here off the golf course. McDuff had said he was some manner of judge or another.

Satisfied that this Fitzsimmons was alone, and perhaps getting a bit impatient, Rory stepped back into the terminal to emerge again three doors down. From there, he made a bold approach, a bag in each hand and a broad, friendly smile on his face.

"Judge Fitzsimmons?"

The big gent straightened, relief, if nothing else, in his expression. "Rory Devaney, I expect?" Rather than offer a hand to a man carrying two bags, he turned to pop the boot lid with a tiny transmitting device attached to his key ring.

Rory tossed one bag into the boot and started around the car to the passenger side door with the other.

"Feel free to toss the other in here, too," the judge offered. "Not like there isn't enough room."

"Rather have it with me," Rory replied, and looked around him. "So this is America."

"No, son. This is Newark. Once you see a bit more of this great land, you'll never confuse the two again. Trust me."

Fitzsimmons had no idea if Rory trusted him. Every fiber of the younger man's being was hyper-alert to movements in his surroundings: studying, weighing, analyzing. His bag wedged between his legs, he watched the judge buckle his shoulder harness and get them underway.

"They tell me you're a jooge." He meant to say it by way of making conversation, but knew that a part of him was asking more. His survival was dependent on the quality of the intelligence he was able to gather, and he was a man addicted to the gathering and assimilation of information. "What sort, if I may be so bold to ask. I don't know many jooges, socially speaking."

Fitzsimmons glanced quickly over. His expression stated plainly that he was unaccustomed to getting the third degree from anyone, let alone a baby-faced blond twenty-eight-year-old. "State Supreme Court, which isn't quite as lofty as it might sound. Criminal cases and civil litigations."

"They tell me your father is from the north."

Fitzsimmons nodded. This was a subject with which he was more comfortable. "Belfast. Fought on the Republic side during the Civil War. Fled here in 1921 after the signing of the Anglo-Irish Treaty. My two uncles didn't, and wound up on a prison ship."

Rory perked up. "Which one? Do y' know?"

"The *El Rahway.*"

"My grand da was on that same ship, and a right bloody hell I've heard it was."

The judge settled back a bit in his seat. Rather than take the Holland Tunnel to Manhattan, he followed signs leading them to the New Jersey Turnpike. Southbound. "So you and I could easily be in each other's shoes today, eh?"

"Y' might say that," Rory supposed, "You were able t' stretch your imagination quite that far. Mine's been pinned to ground, by the jackboot on my neck."

Fitzsimmons didn't bristle, but then he had a genuine Irishman fresh from the conflict in his car. Something deep in him desperately needed to persuade Rory of his own innate Irishness. "You want to know what our single biggest problem here is? Getting all the fat asses living off the prosperity of this land to remember the misery of their own flesh and blood. No man should have to beg money for such a cause as ours."

Ours. This was the immigrant's curse. American Irish who needed to make that connection. For most natives who'd stayed behind, it no longer existed. They were bored with those who made the obligatory pilgrimage back to the old sod, looked up distant relatives oblivious to their existence, and kissed the fucking Blarney Stone. Rory grimaced, bit his tongue, and pretended to be engrossed with the landscape.

"People just don't understand what is going on

over there," Fitzsimmons pressed on. "Not but a handful of us here. Me? I think I understand the troubles pretty well."

Rory couldn't help himself. He tore his gaze from the scenery to fix the judge with the most enigmatic of smiles. "We have a saying, Mr. Fitzsimmons. A bit of a joke, if you will. If you're not confused, you don't know what is going on."

Nonplussed, Fitzsimmons grunted and slapped the wheel with one meaty paw. "It's a horrid, criminal thing they've done to our people. That much I understand. When I think of it, watch the news accounts, and read what I read in the international press, it makes my blood boil. More than once I've been tempted to say the hell with it here, chuck it all, go over there and pick up a gun."

Rory didn't know whether to cheer or choke him. Stupid well-fed ass knew as much about big boys' rules as Rory did about the New York State Criminal Code. He moved hurriedly to change the subject before he lost his temper.

"Tell me about these people I'm staying with, Jooge. How are they connected?"

"They're not," Fitzsimmons replied. "That's the beauty of it. They're clean."

Surprised, Rory realized he was gaping at him, and slowly shut his mouth. "So how do y' know them?"

"I've known Tom O'Meara almost thirty years. He served under my father."

Served. "A soldier?"

"Police officer. He's a cop."

Now Rory was sure the dotty old bleeder had lost his fucking mind. "Let me understand this. You're putting me up with a policeman."

Fitzsimmons beamed over at him, his eye with the twinkle of anything but a crazy man. "Safest place in the city. And his wife is one hell of a cook. I'm not a nutcase, so stop looking at me like that."

Rory asked his next question cautiously. "So what is it you've told them about me?"

"That you're a friend of the family. Trying to make a go of it here."

Thirty minutes into their journey, as they crossed the Goethals Bridge from New Jersey onto Staten Island, Rory gestured to his surroundings. They had suddenly turned much more residential than anywhere in the wasteland they'd just passed through on the other side of the bridge. "Can I assume we're getting close to our destination?"

"Ten minutes, maybe," the judge replied.

"You've got something for me, I think."

Fitzsimmons grunted and nodded. "Under the spare cover, in the trunk."

"What if they come out t' greet us at the house? It could get a bit sticky, me digging into the spare well for a gun and all."

The judge lifted an eyebrow as he glanced Devaney's way. "You're a cautious one, aren't you, son."

Rory stared hard at him. "My da's dead, sir, and I'll thank y' not to call me that. Shot down in cold blood by the fookin' UVF. I've given back some of what he got, and lived t' tell because I'm cautious. It's my middle fookin' name."

Sergeant Tom O'Meara didn't know why he should be anxious tonight, but he was. Judge Pete Fitzsimmons and he went back a long way, to a time when he was a rookie beat cop in Captain Joe Fitzsimmons's Tenth Precinct command. Pete had served as deputy to Manhattan's District Attorney then, and was as much like a big brother to Tom as Joe was like a father. O'Meara was the only child of a widowed immigrant mother and the Fitzsimmonses were like family. So when Pete called last week to ask this favor, what could Tom and Sheila say? Thanks for all those years of ballet tickets—Sheila's passion, not Tom's—and Knicks and Giants tickets, but no thanks? He's a distant relative of yours and no relative of ours, so find him someplace else? Tom couldn't imagine. He had a whole finished basement that was hardly ever used, complete with toilet, shower, and color TV. Whoever the kid was, if he was Fitzsimmons blood from any branch of old Joe's family tree, why shouldn't he be welcome? As long as he kept his hands off Tom's oldest daughter, Bridget.

When the doorbell rang, O'Meara was still in the basement doing last-minute straightening up. He heard his youngest daughter, Annie, call out, "Daddy!", and started for the stairs. In his mind by now, the kid Pete was dumping on them had hairy knuckles that dragged the floor, a deli-size sausage lump in his pants, and the perpetually craven expression of a deviate. Not only was Bridget no longer safe, but neither were pudgy little Morgan and six-year-old Annie.

The reality of what stood waiting to meet Tom O'Meara and his family in their Arden Heights, Staten Island, living room was so far removed from anything his imagination had conjured, that he actually felt himself stop for a beat and almost gape. The young man beside Pete Fitzsimmons was not a gorilla, but an Adonis. Tall and reed slender, with good shoulders and the facial bones of a male model, this guy was a whole other sort of problem than what Tom had anticipated. This one could lash himself to a mast or chain himself to a chair, and still boy-crazy Bridget would pose a problem. And then again, maybe not. Maybe this one was just so good-looking, the whole time he stayed here, little miss hot-to-trot might just cower terrified in her room.

"Tom," Pete greeted him with his typical hale-fellow-well-met bluster. It was one of those things O'Meara had taught himself to look past when dealing with the man. "Meet my cousin's boy, Rory Devaney. Can't tell you how much I appreciate this."

O'Meara strode forward to shake the young man's hand. A clean-cut guy of maybe thirty, he had a strong, manly grip and a direct way of looking you in the eye. "Pleased to meet you, Rory. Long trip?"

The Irishman shrugged his shoulders with a relaxed ease. "Not so bad, I don't think, sir. You've got a lovely house here. This is very kind, y' letting me stay."

Bridget was going to die when she heard that voice, and so might Sheila. "It's Tom," O'Meara told him. "And our pleasure to have you. I and Pete's family go quite a ways back." He stopped to beckon his youngest daughter out from hiding behind the BarcaLounger. "This is my youngest, Annie. Come out from there and say hello to our guest."

Annie popped her head up from behind the chair like a jack-in-the-box. "Hello, guest." And as quickly as she'd appeared, she disappeared again.

Rory laughed and advanced to peer over the chair at the top of her head. "Annie, is it? What a very pretty name. I'd say it suits any girl so pretty as you."

A ham from birth, Annie flopped onto her back as if smitten, hand over her heart, moaned, and then started to giggle. Pete Fitzsimmons, meanwhile, made gestures toward the door. "Tell Sheila I said hello, Tom. I'm sorry, but I do have to run. Got a St. Vinnie's Hospital shindig at eight, and already I'm going to be late."

"Sheila, Morgan, Bridget!" Tom called out as he walked Fitzsimmons to the door. "We have a guest!" He eyed their young visitor's two bags as Pete tugged the knob toward him and stepped through onto the stoop. "This everything?" he asked.

Pete nodded. "Travels light. I like that in a man. And thanks again, Tom. I really do appreciate this."

At that moment, Sheila appeared from the kitchen, hair up and flour dusting her apron. "Hi, Pete," she greeted him. "Sorry you have to run off."

"Me too." He waved, and blew her a kiss. "Save me a weekend once the weather turns cold. We'll sneak off to an island together."

That Pete. What a kidder. By the time Tom turned back from the front door, it seemed Rory and Annie were already fast friends. The Irishman straightened from his crouch alongside the lounger to greet his hostess, while Annie stood beside him, enraptured.

"Rory Devaney, Mrs. O'Meara," he introduced himself and offered his hand. " 'Tis a lovely home you have, ma'am. And a beautiful little girl."

"Careful." Sheila laughed. "Her head swells too big, we won't be able to get her out the door to school in the morning. Are you hungry, Rory? Supper's just ten, maybe fifteen minutes off."

"Something smells wonderful," he replied. "But I don't want t' put y' out, ma'am. It's nice enough, you've let me stay here until I find my feet."

"Nonsense," she scoffed. "You'll eat any meal, you're here when I serve it. Tom, why don't you show him where to put his bags?"

O'Meara would forever marvel at the woman he'd been lucky enough to marry. A successful real estate broker and mother of three, she had an easy way with people that Tom, a career New York cop of thirty years, had worked his ass off to attain. With her dark, mahogany-red hair and sparkling blue eyes, she still had an appeal that could pluck his heartstrings, even after twenty-three years.

Sheila turned to the stairwell to holler up it to the floor above. "Morgan, Bridget. Where are your manners? Get down here. We have a guest." She shrugged to Rory. "Teenagers. I'm hoping it's a form of reversible brain damage, but I'm about to give up."

A slightly pudgy, dark-haired girl of no more than thirteen appeared at the head of the stairs. Walkman in hand, she came bounding down, stripping headphones from her ears. As she spied Rory, she slowed. "I, um, sorry," she apologized, suddenly self-conscious. "Studying. Didn't hear."

"Your math homework, or Rage Against the Machine?" her father wondered. "Rory, this is Morgan," he introduced her. "Our middle girl. Morgan, this is Rory Devaney."

With a gallant directness, Devaney stepped across to offer the blushing girl his hand. She took it hesitantly and shook, unable to meet his direct, amused gaze. "Very pleased t' meet any fan of such a band. Awesome guitar, no?"

Morgan lit like he'd flipped a switch, eyes suddenly aglow as she met his gaze. "The best!" she blurted. "Wow. You know." She turned to frown at her mom and dad. "They don't. They think everything I listen to is stupid."

Devaney patted that hand he held with his other,

let it go, and winked. "They'll come round, I'm sure of it. I think perhaps I'd better go wash up." Tom had moved to grab Rory's bags and he hurried across the room to take one of them.

"Where's Bridge?" Sheila asked Morgan.

"Where do you think? On the phone."

O'Meara led their guest toward the basement stairs, pausing to holler upstairs, "Bridget! Get off the damned phone and come down to help your mother set the table!"

Judge Pete Fitzsimmons had serious misgivings as he drove east across the Verrazano-Narrows Bridge to Brooklyn. If everything he'd heard was true about this lad, McGuire, no matter what his looks belied, he was one rough customer. Tough, and a survivor, to judge by the act, and how far he'd come. Laden with the guilt of his own father for hiding here on these safe, cozy shores while men like McGuire and Martin McDuff fought and died, Pete wanted to do everything he comfortably could. The fact of the matter, though, was that Judge Pete Fitzsimmons was afraid. Afraid of what McGuire, aka Rory Devaney, could do to him here. Frankie McGuire had killed policemen, and Fitzsimmons had moved him in with one, for want of a safer, less likely place. At the time he'd thought of it, the notion had seemed an inspired one. Now, he wondered. Tom O'Meara was an easygoing but competent cop, and no dummy.

Fitzsimmons sighed, shook his head, and checked

the dash clock for the time. Seven twenty-three. He and Juliet were due at that fund-raiser at eight. He was still fifteen minutes from home and not even dressed yet.

4

When he heard he would be living in a basement for the next couple of months, Rory Devaney had his doubts. He'd conjured an image of empty cottage crawl spaces, burned-out safe house cellars, damp dripping walls, and rats. Now, as he descended these stairs to the O'Meara basement, he was more than a little surprised. The walls, floors, and ceiling of that vast, mostly open space were finished just like the rest of the house. There was a big bed, settee, television, and highboy at one end of the room, set off by a shelving unit partition. And at the other end stood a cozy little setup that looked like the bar area in a tiny corner pub.

"The kids were supposed to clear some of this crap out and stack it against that wall," O'Meara complained as he passed a small pile of cardboard cartons. "It's just video games, Annie's coloring books and stuff." He stopped at the foot of the double bed and dropped the bag he carried onto it. "Dresser is empty, along with most of the closet. It's not much, but it's warm and it's dry."

Rory stood surveying his surroundings, barely able to contain his delight. Privacy, more comforts than any home he'd ever had, *and* a bar. "Please. This is grand, Tom."

"That's the bath over there." O'Meara pointed to a door. "Just a shower, not a tub. And you've got to jiggle the handle on the crapper sometimes."

Devaney set the bag he carried alongside the other on the bed. "I suppose I'd better get in there and scrub a little, I want to be presentable for evening nosh, eh? Again, I can't thank y' enough for your hospitality, Tom. You and your wife." He smiled and offered his hand again. "She's lovely, by the way."

"And smart as a whip," O'Meara told him as they shook. "How you fixed for work? Fitz set something up for you?"

"Aye. Says every mick first arrives here does construction labor. Under-the-table money, he calls it. Until I can find something better."

"Whereabouts?" Tom wondered.

"Manhattan. Some outfit with a job on Forty-seventh and Broadway. Big Apple Construction's the name."

Tom wandered across the room to the little bar as they spoke, stepped behind it and stooped to open a tiny refrigerator. From it, he withdrew a pair of bottled beers. "Bud Light is all I've got. Trying to watch the old waistline. It's cold, though."

Devaney had little regard for the tasteless, pasteurized swill that Americans called beer, but the flight had parched him. He was happy to accept O'Meara's offer, and clicked bottles with him once the caps were off. "Cheers," he toasted. Even Budweiser tasted wonderful to him, his mouth was so dry. "This is very decent of you, knowing the reputation us Irish have carried abroad." He nodded toward the bar setup as he spoke. "But I swear I'll not drink you out of house and home."

"My beer is yours," Tom replied. "Feel free to help yourself."

"Daddy," a new voice called to them from upstairs. Light and musical, but more womanly than girlish. "Dinner."

"A quick scrub then," Rory excused himself. "And thanks again, Tom."

"Don't thank me," O'Meara told him. "Thank Fitz."

Bridget O'Meara thought they needed another warm body in their already crowded house like an elephant in the yard. At seventeen, the thing she craved more than anything in life—with the possible exception of Kevin Donohue's undying love and affection—was privacy. An avid reader of romance fiction, Bridget used those silly, predictable plots as a means of escape to tranquil places where her bothersome brat sisters couldn't trespass. It was the same with the basement, where she had come to think of the bathroom and stereo down there as her own, and where she often took her books to escape Morgan's vapid singing to her Walkman. Now the basement had an invader. One who might occupy it for months, she'd been told. An Irish charity case of Uncle Fitz's, undoubtedly old, down on his luck, and probably a drunk. Bridget knew enough of the world to know how most of them were; the ones who came over here from the old sod.

Busy with her mother in the kitchen, spooning boiled cabbage and potatoes into serving bowls, Bridget had her back to the door when their house-guest appeared for dinner. It was his voice she heard first, not at all coarse, as she'd imagined.

"I expect this must be Bridget."

She turned to meet perhaps the most handsome man she'd ever seen, eyeing her in a frank and friendly way. A hot flush of sudden embarrassment burned her face and scalp. Some old drunk.

"Bridget, say hello to Rory Devaney," her mother introduced them.

"H-hi," she stammered, and instantly hated herself for it. How cool. How sophisticated.

"Pleased t' meet y', Bridget." He strode forward to offer his hand as he said it. "Nobody mentioned you're quite so pretty as you are."

More prickles across her scalp as Rory took her hand and shook it. In her mind's eye she could see her face, undoubtedly as bright red as a squalling infant's. Her fair Irish skin often lent itself to such betrayals of her inner discomfort, and right now she wanted to crawl off and die.

"Bridget's a junior at St. John Villa Academy," her mother told Devaney. "Wants to be an actress, but don't they all at her age?"

Rory winked at Bridget. "Then she'll need t' learn t' take the unexpected on the chin and not to blush. I expect she will. Most young women eventually do."

Kill me now, Bridget groaned inwardly. And wondered if a quick, merciful death would be enough.

As he took his place at the O'Meara family table, Rory Devaney reminded himself of who he was in this setting. Even the most harmless flirtation with an impressionable young woman like Bridget O'Meara could be dangerous, not because she could hurt him, but he could hurt her. It was some years since he'd discovered the considerable effect he could have on some women. And over the time since, when his mood and the situation suited, he'd exploited that advantage. Often, he'd done it toward less than noble ends, but then he was a soldier who'd daily risked his life. What sort of future could he promise any woman, regardless of her qualities and expectations? But circumstances here were different. Tom and Sheila O'Meara had offered him the sanctuary of their home, purely because a trusted friend had asked that favor. That made little

Bridget off limits, no matter how pretty and vulner-able to his charms she might be.

Tom asked Annie to say grace, then Sheila asked Rory for his plate. Once she piled it with slices of reddish, boiled meat, he placed it on the table before him and accepted a bowl of boiled spuds.

"Smells wonderful," he complimented his host-ess. "May I ask what it is?"

Sheila glanced at him curiously, almost as if she thought he was toying with her. "Corned beef and cabbage. You're kidding, right?"

He shook his head. "No. Why do you say that?"

"I made it especially for this occasion. We have the impression it's all you eat over there."

"Corned beef you say?" Now *he* felt slightly em-barrassed. "Boiled beef and ham, surely. But corned beef, never. Indeed, I thought ham might be what it is. Save for the texture."

From across the table, Morgan stared open-mouthed at him. "You're from Ireland and you've never had corned beef? That's crazy."

"Sorry," he replied. "Never even seen it before." And as he spoke he lifted a first forkful to his mouth. Falling-apart tender, with a faint pickled, briny taste, it was more palatable than any ordinary boiled beef he'd had. "Umm, delicious."

"Oh," Tom exclaimed from the head of the table, suddenly rising. "I almost forgot." He hurried from the room to return a moment later with two bottles of Guinness Extra Stout and a pair of frosted mugs. "You do have this over there, don't you?"

Rory grinned as bottle and mug were set before him. "Aye. This I was baptized in."

Annie turned in her seat beside him to stare at him in astonishment. "In Ireland, they baptize you with beer?"

As everyone at the table roared with laughter, Rory was conscious of how Bridget kept stealing glances at him. Not this one, he warned himself. Best behavior, mate.

5

◆

Last night, before he turned in to get some much-needed sleep, Rory had told Tom O'Meara he was expected on the job site at eight in the morning. He wondered how early he would have to leave to get there from Arden Heights using public transportation. On the map of the city that Tom gave him, it looked like half a day's journey, at least, and Rory was grateful when O'Meara offered him a ride. A uniformed sergeant who worked out of the Thirty-fourth Precinct in the Inwood area of Manhattan, Tom worked the eight-to-four shift. He'd assured Rory that as long as he didn't mind reporting a few minutes early, dropping him midtown would be his pleasure.

Rather than take the ferry that ran from St.

George Station to the South Ferry terminal,
O'Meara opted to drive the Verrazano-Narrows
bridge and run north to the Brooklyn Battery Tunnel. On that crisp, cloudless autumn morning, with
the harbor waters sparkling below, Rory felt almost
too much at peace to be such a stranger in this
strange land. The bridge structure itself was like
none he'd ever seen, but in pictures. Awesome in its
height, span, and mass, it was just the sort of thing
he expected of America, where in his imagination,
everything was bigger than life. It was from that
span that he caught his first glimpse of Manhattan,
again pleased to see its sheer mass was everything
he'd dreamed.

"It still gets me, too," Tom murmured, observing
Rory's reaction to the sight. "And I've lived here all
my life. It's even more impressive at night."

"I'll bet," Rory enthused. "There are the World
Trade Towers, right where they're supposed t' be.
And even the spire of the Empire State Buildin',
beyond."

"You build 'em that big, they're kinda hard to
move," O'Meara joked. "By the way. I meant to ask
last night. How you set for cash?"

"I'm fine. Changed a few quid for dollars at the
airport," Rory lied. "They'll hold me, I'm sure,
until I get paid."

Tom nodded, satisfied. "You need a bridge loan, I
want you to feel free to ask. Hear?"

"I'm grateful, Tom, but I'm fine. Truly I am." It

felt strange enough to be riding in a car with a cop-
per, resplendent in serious dark uniform, those three
bright blue stripes on his sleeve. But to have him
offer to loan him money, out of obvious concern for
his well-being. That topped it all. O'Meara liked
him. He felt confident of that fact. And cop or not,
he couldn't help but like the man in return.

"You remembered that map, and know how to get
back now?" Tom asked as they entered the tunnel.

Rory patted the front pocket of his dungarees. "I
did and I do. Sheila said supper's at six. Unless I
end up in the Bronx, I'll try to be on time."

Rory Devaney waited until Tom O'Meara was well
on his way back west toward the Henry Hudson
Parkway before he sauntered casually away from
that construction site on the corner of Forty-seventh
Street and Broadway. According to Fitz, his name
would appear on the Big Apple Construction lists as
undocumented day labor, should anyone check with
their front office. If someone tried to reach him at
the site, he was off helping expedite materials.

The sheer volume of pedestrian traffic on Times
Square was something for which even Rory's fertile
imagination couldn't prepare him. An impossibly
tall woman, on the arm of a distinguished-looking
white-haired gent, was dressed in a little sheath so
scrupulously cut, it fitted to her every spectacular
jut and curve. She reminded him of just how long it
had been since he was last in the company of a
woman. For the two months he'd spent on the lam,

he'd lived like a monastic. Two months was too long for a young man of his appetites and drive.

At the corner of Forty-second Street and Seventh Avenue, Rory descended stairs to a token booth, and purchased the fare for the Seventh Avenue–Broadway Local. This was exactly as he'd imagined it would be, having seen the subways of New York in Hollywood movies. The heavy steel girders, beams, and columns, painted with a hundred coats of shiny enamel. Tracks and tunnel walls covered with soot. Platforms jammed with commuters of every race and nationality. Rory believed he'd never been anywhere more alive than the throbbing heart of this vast metropolis. The intensity of sheer sensory bombardment was almost overwhelming. When the doors of his train opened, he boarded it and grabbed a handhold, grateful for that anchor in this sea. It was something one grew accustomed to, he knew, but right now he was dizzy.

The terminus of the Number One local's run was South Ferry. That was where Rory disembarked to walk counter to the flow of commuters toward the Staten Island Ferry. It would appear that the entire population of Staten Island all worked in Manhattan, and all of them were running late this morning. A virtual horde surged past him, each eye set arrow-straight on some unseen, distant prize. That first cup of coffee. The unconsummated stock deal. Rest for a tired backside and sore feet.

Rory had purchased ferry fare and passed beyond yet another turnstile when suddenly he was jostled rudely from his right and pushed in the path of a pretty blonde.

"Hey!" she snarled on collision. "Watch where you're going, asshole!"

"I apologize," Rory murmured, and whirled to learn who had hip-checked him like that.

"Wouldn't have the time, would y', Goldilocks?" Sean Geary leered at the blonde.

"Fuck yourself," she spat, and stalked off.

Sean smiled broadly at Rory and gave him a lazy, philosophical shrug. "Too tall for me, and too stuck-up for you anyway, Frankie boy."

"I'm not the asshole, you are," Devaney complained. "And it's Rory, y' bloody berk, not Frankie."

"Fuck sakes. It's good t' see you, too," Geary grumbled as he fell in step beside his old mate.

"Y' almost gave me a bloody heart attack, Seanie. What the fook y' wearin', for jaysus sake." Rory surveyed the getup Geary sported with a disdainful shake of the head. "Y' look like a nancy-boy in that rig."

The shorter, wiry Sean Geary stepped ahead of Devaney to hold open the front of his sport coat and twirl. "It's called style, mate. Calvin fookin' Klein."

Rory surveyed the woven loafers, shiny silk blend trousers, and collarless shirt. "Y' look more like a fookin' circus Klein t' me. Them don't hardly look like work clothes."

Sean smirked. "Y'er right. They're not."

They rode one of the golden-yellow ferries back across the harbor, past the fabled Statue of Liberty, to the terminal at St. George Station. All the while, Sean regaled Rory with stories of his own arrival on these shores, four weeks back. To hear him tell it, the women here were so loose they practically stripped off their knickers and jumped you on the sidewalk. Most of the beer was god-awful, fast food was the Lord's gift to humankind, and nights were better than days, with Manhattan clubs staying open until dawn. Back on dry land, Sean led the way up the access ramp to the street with the cocky confidence of an old hand at all this. Four weeks, and to listen to him he was practically a native.

On the street, Geary led Rory toward one of the vast public parking lots, several blocks west. A hundred yards from their destination, Sean spotted an empty soda can and nudged it atop his foot like a soccer ball. "Still got the moves?" he challenged his friend.

"Try me," Rory growled.

Sean feinted left, then dribbled the can right to slip past Rory's guard, but Devaney was having none of it. A leg tackle sent Geary skidding, more concerned about his threads than the can, and Rory picked him clean. For the next eighty yards, Sean feinted and attacked like a terrier as Rory moved the can down the lane of parked cars. Once, he managed to steal it, but only for an instant before the bigger, more skilled Devaney darted a foot in to snatch it back. When Sean finally pulled up, winded, Rory took aim and booted the can harder than he intended into the rear quarter of a parked Pontiac Sunbird.

"Goal!"

"Hey!" Sean complained. "Watch it. That's my fookin' car." He hurried forward to examine the small chip in the paint the can had made, and reached to polish it with the sleeve of his jacket.

"Your car." Rory was panting, too, and had his hands on his knees to catch his breath.

"Bought and paid for. Ain't she grand?"

As much as Rory wanted to say that it looked like just another car to him, he was impressed that Sean had been able to come this far, so fast. He'd had doubts about the wisdom of sending Geary here first, as a sort of advance man. Now, it was looking as though his doubts were unfounded. Less dependent on Fitzsimmons's American support machine by design, he'd managed to find a place to live, learn the ropes of this intimidating metropolis, and buy himself a shiny little car, virtually on his own.

"Aye," Rory replied. "Grand, indeed. And I'll bet she's gonna take us to a boatyard."

Sean removed a ring of keys from his jacket pocket, and now he paused. "We're really gonna do this, Frankie?"

His thoughts drawn far away to an island across the same waters that lapped these shores, Rory stared unseeing at those twin towers of the World Trade Center, just opposite. "Indeed we are, Sean. Either that, or die glorious deaths trying."

* * *

Each morning, they lined up five abreast to fill the room Sergeant Tom O'Meara now addressed from his podium. Baby-faced kids, fresh out of junior college and the academy. Grizzled veterans who'd barely finished high school. Everything in between. They were shorter on the whole than they were when O'Meara first came up, before the Knapp Commission and a legion of civil rights lawsuits. More women, African-Americans, Hispanics, Orientals. More Jews and Eastern Europeans, too. Fewer Irish and Italians, but still more of them than anyone else. Former Mayor David Dinkins, a piss-poor policeman's friend if ever there was one, had tried to insist that New York was not a melting pot but a beautiful mosaic. Like hell, was Tom O'Meara's response to that notion. It was either a melting pot or a sadly lost cause. Old Dave had never carried a gun on his hip and tried to walk a beat in this town.

"Zito," his voice boomed out.

"Here."

"Gaines."

"Present."

Tom looked up at the blue-jawed Larry Zito and acne-scarred Lucy Gaines. "You two are sector Adam. Vermilyea to the park. Thirteen hundred meal." He glanced back at his roster. "Walker."

"Here."

"Gomez."

"Here."

"You're sector David. Thirteen hundred meal.

Everybody else, same posts and meals as posted. By the way, if you haven't qualified yet, get your butt to the range. It's available to all Manhattan North uniformed personnel for the next four days. Lieutenant?"

Lieutenant Roy Bascom, tall and impeccably turned out in a crisp white shirt that contrasted with his ebony skin, stepped forward from the side of the room, clipboard in hand. "We're working two cars short today, so keep your heads up, people. Who's got house duty?"

"I do," Barbara Miller replied.

"Try to keep one eye on the cars at the curb if you can," Bascom told her. "Some crack wacko's been stealing wiper blades."

O'Meara and Bascom stepped away from the podium together as horseplay stirred the back of the room. Tom looked up to see Marty O'Brien passing his hat. Marty met his eye and grinned.

"We're taking up a collection, Sarge. Everybody dig deep. Cop in distress. My five bucks is already in there, for the Edwin Diaz Driver Training Fund."

Hoots and whistles erupted as other cops rained a torrent of singles and loose change down on the hat.

"Make sure they start him off with training wheels," somebody shouted.

"Hell no! One o' them simulators is a better idea!"

O'Meara's partner, Eddie Diaz, rolled his eyes and shook his head. "I can drive and you assholes know it," he grumbled.

"Yeah, and he has his learner's permit in his wallet to prove it," a voice shot back.

"You've had your fun," O'Meara chided good-naturedly. Gesturing with both hands, he shooed them from the room. "Let's hit the bricks. Make Inwood safe for democracy."

Later, as Tom and Eddie walked toward their squad car, Diaz let loose with the same complaint Tom heard now with numbing regularity.

"This is getting ridiculous, boss."

"No more ridiculous than it was last week. You ask them to check that tire pressure last night?"

"Yeah, yeah. Look, boss. I'm supposed t' drive the car. You s'pose to sit next to me and ride around like all the other boss cops do. That's the pass them stripes bought you. And the other way around, it just don't look right."

Tom shrugged. "You've probably got a point."

"So?"

"I'll drive, you ride."

Diaz slapped his hat against his thigh. "Oh, man. What's the cop teamed with a sergeant called? His driver, right?"

"Absolutely."

"And ain't that what the duty sheet designates me?"

"Right again."

They reached their car, and O'Meara held his hand out for the key.

"So what the fuck, Sarge?" Eddie complained. "When you gonna start lettin' me do my job?"

Tom tilted his head and gave him his best lepre-chaun smile. "How about tomorrow?"

"Shit," Eddie grumbled, and started around the front of the car toward the passenger side. "You been sayin' that going on three years."

6

The boatyard was located on Arthur Kill in the northern reaches of Staten Island's Tottenville section. From Rory's perspective it was blessedly convenient; just a Staten Island Rapid Transit Railway ride from the Annadale Station, only a mile from the O'Meara's Arden Heights home. But that was the only thing at all blessed about this situation. The boat that Sean had located and purchased with funds from the Provisional IRA's limited war chest, was a wreck.

"Sweet Jesus Lord," Rory complained as he contemplated the craft. An ancient oceangoing tug designed for shoal waters and close-in coastal salvage work, it had not just seen better days, but better decades. Its battered hull was one huge scab of rust, probably plucked from the sea by a crane twenty years ago and left here to rot.

"Here it is," Sean declared proudly. "The Irish Republic Navy's fleet. Though I do admit she needs a bit of work."

"A bit?" Rory asked, incredulous. "Even if she'd float, look at the fookin' prop. Every blade bent to hell, like the whole goddamn vessel was dropped on her arse."

Geary shrugged. "So the pitch is a bit off. We'll have t' pull it."

"An open ocean voyage clear back to Ireland requires a dependable engine, Seanie. This boat's diesel is most likely scrap, just like the rest of her."

"Now y'er startin' to hurt my feelin's, Frankie. They and it aren't any such thing."

Devaney spun on him. "The next time y' call me that, I'm gonna fookin' shoot you, Sean. Last warning. It's Rory. Got it?"

Geary stepped back a pace, hand over his heart. "Shoot me, will y'? And then where would y' be, Rory Devaney? Y' helped your da tend his boat as a boy. I worked six years as an apprentice mechanic and two as a journeyman in the Belfast shipyard. She may look like a wreck but she in't, or I would'na bought her."

Rory looked away to survey the tug once again, unwilling to push his friend further. They were all alone in this together, just the two of them. They'd been through much worse than getting some sad wreck of a boat in shape. He had to remember that.

"Y' think she'll even float?" he asked, tone heavy with doubt.

"I been over every square inch of her skin with a hammer. No holes, and not even any terrible thin spots. A few places, we'll want t' weld plate to the hull from the inside. We sandblast and lay on a coat of epoxy paint, she'll give us at least another knot, knot and a half."

"When do we start?" Rory asked.

Sean eyed his work clothes and boots. "Y' want to arrive home filthy, do y' not? So your people'll buy that construction cover Fitzsimmons gave y'. The deck and wheelhouse look like a rubbish dump. Why don't we start now?"

"And you dressed like that? What'll you do? Point?"

Geary smirked and let his eyes drift over the battered old tug's lines. "It's a thought. But naw. I've got my duffel of work duds in the boot."

Eddie Diaz had this thing for fried food, and Tom O'Meara had spent the last three years trying to break him of it. Eddie argued that his tastes were cultural, which made any attempt to dissuade him from them politically incorrect. O'Meara had wondered aloud on more than one occasion how politically correct a heart attack at age forty-five might be, but Eddie continued to turn a deaf ear. Each day for lunch, while O'Meara ate things like carrots, apples, celery, and cabbage from the brown bag he prepared himself each morning, Diaz insisted they

stop at a fried chicken joint, Burger King, or
Cucchifrito stand. Like a Whopper was part of his
Latino heritage.

Today's choice was fried chicken, and while Tom
sat behind the wheel of the cruiser, Eddie ran inside
to pick up the order he'd phoned in half an hour ago.
Tom munched on a quarter head of raw cabbage and
thought less about what it would do toward scrub-
bing carcinogens from his colon than he did about
last night. Sheila had been even more worried about
Rory Devaney than he had been. Inviting a strange
man into a house with three daughters got the
mother bear working in her. But as soon as she saw
the easy way he'd kidded with Annie, her heart had
melted. The fact that he was such a good-looking
bastard couldn't have hurt his chances either. Sheila
always did have an eye for male beauty. She'd married it, hadn't she?

No matter how deep he let himself go in his dis-
tractions, the natural-born street cop in Tom
O'Meara never seemed to sleep. Out of one corner
of his eye, he was forever tracking action on the
street around him. The instant he spotted the young
kid in full sprint down the sidewalk opposite, he
checked first for pursuit, then reached for the ignition key. Fifty feet behind the kid, Walker and
Gomez were hot on his tail, the black cop keeping
pace while the overweight Ignacio rapidly gave
ground. Tom had the engine started and was ready
to swing the cruiser round through the first break in
traffic when Eddie Diaz bolted from the chicken

joint to toss his lunch order in through the open passenger window.

"I'm on 'im, boss," he shouted. For a guy who ate all that fried food, Diaz could fly. Equipment belt and all, he took off down that sidewalk at a flat-out run.

O'Meara, meanwhile, saw his break develop in traffic, hit the lights and gunned it around while the suspect disappeared at 190th Street into tiny Gorman Memorial Park. No fool, Tom turned a hard right on 187th Street, and then a quick left a block later at Wadsworth Avenue. Sprinting out the other side of Gorman Park, the kid was looking behind him, with both Walker and Eddie Diaz hot on his trail. At the corner of 190th Street and Wadsworth Terrace, O'Meara jerked the car up over the curb and diagonally across the sidewalk to block the boy's path. Preoccupied with being caught from behind, the kid never saw the squad car until he heard the tires squeal. He turned, and slammed full-tilt into the right front fender. Then he collapsed on the pavement in a heap.

"Dumb shit," Tom muttered. He grabbed his nightstick off the floor and opened his door.

By the time O'Meara rounded the back end of the car, Jerry Walker had the perp thrown over the hood and pinned there while a panting Eddie Diaz threw cuffs on him.

"I didn't do nothing wrong, let me go!" the kid hollered.

By the look of him, O'Meara judged his age to be

no more than fourteen or fifteen. "He got a wallet on him?" Tom asked Walker. "What's the story?"

"My rookie partner saw him hijack somethin' from a bodega at Broadway and One Ninety-third," Jerry Walker explained. He watched as Diaz jerked the kid upright and patted his pockets for a wallet. His hands stopped on an object in the right front pocket.

"What's your name, son?" O'Meara asked the suspect.

"Carlos."

"Carlos who?"

"DeLaveaga. I ain't never done nothing wrong, I swear. Lemme go."

Eddie dug the object out of the kid's pants pocket. A three-pack of condoms. "Well lookee here. Long Dong's lifesavers. Looks like grand larceny t' me."

O'Meara's radio squawked a status request from the captain with the duty, back at the station house. Tom raised it to his mouth and thumbed the transmit button. "O'Meara here. We're all clear, Cap." He could hear two sirens in the distance. "Units break off. Resume patrol. Over."

One hand clutching his side, rookie P.O. Ignacio Gomez staggered onto the scene from across Wadsworth Terrace. "My bust, Sarge," he called out. "I witnessed the snatch."

Tom lifted his eyes heavenward. "It's a two dollar ninety-eight cent pack of rubbers, for crissake. For this, four sworn officers of the law risk their lives. I risk twenty thousand dollars' worth of taxpayers' property, and the lives of pedestrians, as I give chase in hot pursuit." He stopped to stare hard at the panting rookie. "Does any of this make sense to you, Officer Gomez?"

"But . . ." Gomez started to protest.

"Fucking bust-crazy bullshit," Eddie Diaz snarled at him. "That's all it is and you know it. What? You think you gonna make detective in a week? Use your fucking *cabeza*." He tapped his head hard with an index finger.

O'Meara faced young Carlos DeLaveaga. "How old are you, Carlos?"

The kid mumbled, "Fifteen."

Christ. Two years younger than Bridget and he was out risking his life stealing rubbers. "Don't you know, you run from the cops, you risk getting your ass shot?"

DeLaveaga stared at the tops of his sneakers. "My girlfriend, she said she won't do it without those," he explained, his voice barely above a whisper. "But I buy them, everyone thinks I'm *maricón.*"

O'Meara reflected on the twisted world they all lived in. How old was this girl who wouldn't do it without rubbers, he wondered? Morgan's age? And what sort of society was so twisted up with homophobia that it would rather its men risk HIV infection than risk the appearance of being gay? There were times when he wondered if he was wasting his time out here.

"Cut him loose," he ordered Diaz. With the hand

that held the packet of condoms, he lifted Carlos DeLaveaga's chin to look him straight in the eye. "Get out of here, son. I don't ever want to see you in trouble again."

The kid nodded, reached for the condoms, and Tom grabbed his hand. "You got shit for brains? Don't get greedy. I said go."

Rather than run, DeLaveaga turned to saunter off. This was his neighborhood, and residents of nearby buildings were watching the drama unfold from every available window. A young stud had his image to maintain.

"Hey!" O'Meara called out to him.

For a beat, it looked like the kid might bolt. Then he stopped and slowly turned. "Wha?"

"These are dangerous times. Your girlfriend is right." Tom tossed him the pack of rubbers.

For eight hours Rory Devaney had slaved over the deck of that tug, tossing debris to the ground around it, scraping at the rust-blistered paint of the wheelhouse, and washing down every surface he could reach with the power washer Sean had purchased. Three times that day, a grease-smeared Geary had emerged from the engine compartment below to drive off in his car, each time returning with some part his labors demanded. Once, he'd returned with sandwiches of something called pastrami, a meat that closely resembled the corned beef that Sheila O'Meara had served Rory last night. Now, as he climbed up the ladder from the ground and hauled himself over the boat's port gunwale, he brandished an engine belt of some sort, and a six-pack of beer.

"Cheers, mate," he greeted his filthy comrade. "Time t' call it a day."

"Those cold?" Rory asked. His throat was so parched from old paint and rust dust, he wasn't sure it really mattered if they were or not.

"As a Rocky Mountain stream" Sean drawled in a poor imitation of a Western cowboy accent. He'd clearly spent his idle time watching too much American television.

Rory dragged over a crate to sit and survey the results of his labors as his mate twisted caps off a pair of bottles. More Budweiser, Devaney noticed. While he hoped he wouldn't be here long enough to actually get used to that swill, he accepted the offered bottle graciously. "Thanks. Cheers."

"So tell me about this place you're in. The one Fitzsimmons found you," Sean prodded. He sank to the deck, back propped against the wheelhouse bulkhead.

"He's a cop."

That got his attention. "You're joking."

"No. Nice enough bloke though, it seems. Lovely wife. Nice family. A life like his must be easy enough t' live."

Sean stared down the length of the deck toward the stern. "So. Y' still feel as negative about this old girl as y' did this morning. We made progress today."

It would have been an exaggeration to say the

deck gleamed, but even when the boat was in service, it probably hadn't looked this clean. A little more scraping and paint, Rory thought he could even grow fond of the craft. He'd been a sucker for boats all his life, and Sean had been right about this one. She wasn't pretty, but her hull was sound. A few more weeks' labor like the day they'd just put in, she would be seaworthy. The only remaining question in Rory's mind was, would her engines run?

"How did it go below?" he asked.

Sean shrugged. "Crankshaft is sound. All the pistons run smooth in their sleeves. Entire fuel system's full of condensation and sludge. I've been tinkerin' down there for two weeks, slowly bringin' em' back to operational."

"Any notion why they took her out of service in the first place?" Rory asked.

"The log books say her screw hit a big rock in shoal waters off Block Island. Workin' salvage when a coastwise oil barge went aground. Yardmaster says the owner was near bankruptcy. By the time they got her to dry dock, he didn't deem it worth wastin' his money t' fix her."

"So here she sat?"

"That's right. Until she heard our call t' arms."

"How much fuel she carry?" Rory asked. "Y' said she only did shoal work."

Sean stood, took another sip of his beer and pointed at a pile of old heating oil drums. "Y' see them? I bought 'em off a scrap dealer, up the road in New Dorp. She carries a thousand gallons as it is. With them added, she'll hold three. We could run her clear t' fookin' China."

"Or the north coast of Ireland, at least."

"Aye. Right into Portrush, and the missiles from there, t' shoot right up the British Army's arse. How crazy is that, mate?"

Devaney chuckled. "It's fookin' mad is what it is." And as he stared unseeing into the distance, his expression slowly changed. His jaw set with determination, he spoke through clenched teeth. "That's why it might work."

Patrolman Jerry Walker stood at his locker at end of the shift and hung his equipment belt on its usual hook. The bulletproof vest went in next, while behind him, other cops on the eight-to-four joked and laughed. A lot of this daily letting off steam covered their quiet, unspoken relief. Another day spent in the trenches, another day closer to getting your twenty in and getting the hell out of the line of fire.

"Hey, Walker," Tony Guidetti called out. "I hear the rook confiscated some heavy-duty swag, and O'Meara let the perp walk."

"Some damned fine police work," Walker quipped back. "The new kid's got that ol' eagle eye."

"Shit," Ignacio Gomez complained. Stripped down to an undershirt and boxers, there was no hiding the lousy shape he was in. A layer of baby fat jiggled when he moved. "I was s'pose to do what? Look the other way?"

"Not Ramses, King of the Trojans," Eddie Diaz jeered.

"Ramses was Egyptian," Gomez shot back. "And breaking the law is breaking the law."

Diaz turned away from his locker and squared up to face the kid. "The sarge saved you from yourself, man. He let you make that arrest, pretty soon you're writing up old men for spitting on the sidewalk."

"Boy needs to learn not to run from the police," Gomez defended himself. "I see him do that, I assume he's got something else going maybe. A suspect exhibits suspicious behavior, it's our job to roust him."

"You noticed who did all the roustin'," Jerry Walker growled to Diaz. He turned to his partner. "You wanna be a superhero, son, you're gonna wanna get some of that lead outta your ass. Eddie and the sarge weren't on the scene, I'm left hangin' in the breeze, hotshot."

Ignacio let it roll like water off a ship's deck. "It was a judgment call. I'm still not sorry I made it."

Diaz snorted. "Like the one you made when you bought that piece of shit vest you're wearing? How much more would a good one cost you? A hundred bucks? Or couldn't you find a good one that'd fit?"

Down the hall and around the corner from the patrolmen's locker room, Tom O'Meara sat in a BarcaLounger with an ice bag on his right knee. Back in high school he'd hurt it playing football and had surgery. Orthopedics hadn't made the advances back then that it had since, and one of these days he meant to have an arthroscopic procedure done, to clean up the calcification. The problem was finding the time.

Detective Sergeant Art Dooley slammed the door of his locker and snapped the padlock, then reached for his jacket. They'd been talking about Ignacio Gomez, what had gone down on 190th Street and Wadsworth Terrace that afternoon, and how recruiting objectives had changed within the department over the past decade.

"I dunno. I ain't sayin' I don't think this two years of junior college requirement ain't a good one. It weeds out some of the meatheads," Dooley said. "But back when you and me came up, most guys had a little military experience."

"And a lot more common sense, it seems to me," O'Meara replied. "Gomez had to know that kid might run, and if he did, there wasn't any way he could catch him. You can't leave your partner exposed like that."

Dooley sighed and shook his head. "You seen his file? Straight A's in the Queens College criminology program. Psych profile well within the parameters. Maybe he just needs some time to get his sea legs."

O'Meara shifted the ice bag and grunted. "Jerry Walker should pray he lives that long. G'night, Art."

Dooley paused as he reached the door. "How's that wheel?"

Tom shrugged and smiled. "It's fine. I'm getting too old for this bullshit. Lately, I've been dreaming how it might feel to bake it in some hot, Florida sun."

Dooley, who had five fewer years than Tom's own thirty, had put in for retirement and was moving to West Palm next month. It seemed like everyone O'Meara knew from the old days had moved to either Florida or Myrtle Beach.

"Quit dreaming and do it, Tommy boy." Art disappeared into the hallway outside as he spoke. "You and Sheila come down, I'll have plenty of tequila, margarita mix, and ice."

7

◆

All the way home from Inwood to Arden Heights that evening, O'Meara thought about the twinge he'd felt in his knee, jumping out of the squad car that afternoon. He *was* getting too old for chasing fifteen-year-olds, and wrestling drug-pumped young bucks across tenement rooftops. But if he threw his papers in tomorrow, what would he do with the days, months, and years after that? He was a fifty-two-year-old man with a six-year-old daughter and a vivacious, self-directed forty-three-year-old wife. Sheila had quit her career as a buyer for Macy's in order to have kids, and had only jumped back into the pool two years ago. She sold real estate now, loved it, and was making as much money as he was. If he retired, it would be on almost three-quarters pay, state tax exempt. Almost fifty thousand bucks a year. But with Bridget soon headed off to college, and Morgan right at her heels, that fifty grand wouldn't get them very far. Tom would need to find another job, and not as a security guard at some Palm Beach shopping arcade.

Sheila reported that Rory Devaney had come home head-to-toe filthy just twenty minutes before Tom arrived himself. The young man was downstairs in the shower, told that dinner would be served at six. That kind of dirt meant their guest had put in a good day's work, and O'Meara was pleased to hear it. So many of the Irish who immigrated here today were looking for streets paved with gold and the easy life. If Rory was a worker, not afraid to blister his hands, he'd be fine.

"Bridget's been on the phone for an hour," Sheila complained as Tom started up the stairs to change his clothes. "Maybe she'll listen to you. I can't seem to penetrate."

He smiled and brushed the side of a thumb across her soft, sculpted cheek. After twenty years of marriage and three kids, she was still beautiful. "It's the same thing all mothers and teenage daughters go through, Sheel. You've got two more after her, so brace yourself."

She caught his hand to squeeze it. "Love me?"

"You know I do. What's for dinner?"

"Spaghetti and meatballs. Probably more Irish than we thought corned beef was."

He chuckled, and she slapped his ass as he started to move on. At the head of the stairs, he heard

Bridget's voice in a hushed, excited conversation behind her closed bedroom door. It wasn't his policy to barge in on his kids, but an hour was blatant phone abuse. He rapped twice on the panel and turned the knob to poke his head in.

". . . my sister Morgan's got a crush on him already."

Bridget cupped a hand over the mouthpiece and scowled at the intrusion. "Daddy! I know. I'll be off in a minute."

"Nice to see you, too," he replied. "Five more and I pull the plug, princess. No joke. Then you get your butt downstairs and help your mom with the table."

Her eyes rolled in exasperation, but she was back at it before Tom was half out the door. "Of course he's cute, I guess. But he's old. I don't know. Thirty? That's ancient, Holly."

Apparently, the grapevine was discussing the particulars of the O'Mearas' new lodger. On the one hand, Tom was relieved to hear how disinterested Bridget was claiming to be in Rory Devaney. On the other, if Rory was ancient at thirty, how the hell old was he?

Part of the ritual of putting Annie to bed was the story she demanded her daddy tell her before he could turn out the light. If Tom was really whipped, and pitched his sell job just right, he could on occasion get away with *Curious George* or *The Cat in the Hat.* But most nights, Annie liked the stories he made up off the top of his head. It was the same thing O'Meara's own dad had done for him and his sister as kids, sometimes letting an outlandish story line wind on for months on end. For the past two weeks, Tom had been working the saga of Crusty Crow and Farmer Frowny. Pretty soon, either Crusty would have to move on, or Frowny was finally going to shoot him. Besides, old Crow had eaten just about everything a farmer could conceivably grow. Shiitake mushrooms were about all Tom had left.

"I hate to do this to you," Sheila said as O'Meara crept quietly from his sleeping little girl's room. "But we're out of milk. I guess I forgot to put it on the list."

He slipped an arm around her shoulders and squeezed. "Crazy as the Santangelos have made you with that house they're buying, I can't imagine why. Don't worry about it. You still got work to do?"

She jammed a hand into the back pocket of his jeans to tweak him, and nodded. "Too much. I finally got those Hartley contracts, and the closing's day after tomorrow."

"We getting rich?" he asked.

"I stay on this hot streak, it won't be long. But you know the real estate market. It seems it's always either feast or famine."

It had cooled down enough that evening for Tom to put on a jacket before heading out to the store. He was halfway across the veranda, still zipping it up, when he spotted Rory Devaney on the porch swing.

"Hey, tag along?" he asked. "I'm headed to the store for milk. Nice enough night, I thought I'd walk."

Devaney stood and buttoned his leather jacket. "The store y' say? I was just contemplating tryin' t' find a pub hereabouts. Have a jar or two of stout."

Tom started down the stoop with Rory at his side. "Don't know about stout, but Tiny's over on the next block always has decent ale. After the day it looks like you had, a couple cold ones probably wouldn't hurt you."

"Aye. A couple at least."

As they wandered south down the sidewalk, a neighbor tinkering under the hood of his car hailed O'Meara and waved.

"Hey, Charlie," Tom called back. "Nice night. You need a hand?"

"Naw, Tom. Thanks, I'm about ready t' call the junkyard, have 'em tow this piece of shit away."

Half a block further along, Rory glanced over. "Y' know most of your neighbors, here on the street, do y', Tom?"

"Been here twenty-three years, come February," O'Meara replied. "Seen a few die; others move in or out. But yeah. We know most of them. They like having a cop on the block."

Rory waved a hand back toward the direction they'd come. "Sitting there on your swing, I was thinking to myself how much different this is than anything I'm accustomed to. So peaceful like. I haven't known peace since I was a wee small boy."

"It's really that bad?" O'Meara was so used to the media making mountains out of molehills all over the globe, it was hard to know how bad any situation really was anymore. Starvation in Somalia, genocide in Rwanda, and all those atrocities in Bosnia were fact, he had little doubt. But having seen the way television coverage twisted the face of every fact reported here in his own land, how could he believe he'd been fed the whole truth in each of those places, either? Everyone had an agenda. Why should a news organization, vulnerable to political pressures, and money pressure from their commercial sponsors, be any different?

"Bloody awful," Rory replied. "There's been so much violence, and so many promises made and broken. The only way t' keep your wee arse out of it anymore is t' leave."

"You think the troubles could ever be resolved?" Tom asked.

Devaney grunted. "Who's going to' break down, Tom? It's like a fight between two buck deer in the woods. That's how driven the blood lust has gotten. One side has t' beat the other into submission, I think. How, or when, I don't know. They've been tryin' t' do it to our lot for eight hundred years."

With a gallon of milk in a paper bag, O'Meara led the way from the neighborhood deli-grocery to Tiny's Tavern on Woodrow Road, two blocks from his house. At only a few minutes after eight, it was crowded with the usual mix of neighborhood regulars. This part of Staten Island, between Arden Heights to the west and Annadale to the southeast, was mostly a bedroom community of blue- and white-collar commuters. There were quite a number of cops and firemen living throughout the area, as well as other city workers. Generally, the borough voted Republican, most elections, and resented the rest of the city for voting Democrat. A few years back, they'd tried to secede and incorporate independently. That effort had failed.

"Brace yourself," Tom murmured to Rory as they pushed past the tavern's front door. "The mick-wop rivalry gets a little intense in here sometime. They get a load of that accent, it's sure to fan the flames."

Rory grinned back at him, a strange little twinkle in his eye. "How quaint."

Tom led the way to an empty space at the bar. All stools were taken, but a bunch of regulars were grouped up down at one end, poring over parlay cards and picking the wagers they'd make on that weekend's college and NFL action.

"You're outta your mind," one patron admonished another. "Ain't no fuckin' way the Steelers can cover a ten-point spread. They played like dog-shit last week."

"Against Arizona?" the other man argued back. "They could field their cheerleading squad and still win by twenty points."

Tom grinned as he removed a twenty from his wallet and slapped it on the mahogany. A tall, thin man in a wet apron with rheumy red eyes ap-

proached down the duckboards, and Tom brightened
further. "Tony Baloney. Meet my friend Rory Devaney."

"Any friend of the sarge is a friend of mine, pal,"
Tony said as he shook Rory's hand. "Pleased t'
meetcha. How the hell you been, Sarge?"

"Keeping busy," Tom told him. "What kind of
dark beer you got on tap?"

"Newcastle."

Tom raised a questioning eyebrow to Rory and
saw his eyes flash fire.

"I'd rather drink your Budweiser than that
fookin' Brit swill."

Whoops. "Two Buds," O'Meara told the barkeep.

"Comin' up. I like a man who knows who he
hates. I guess with an accent like that, you ain't one
of the Sarge's old pals, huh?"

Rory smiled. "No. I'd think not. A friend of the
family, come over from the old country."

"And recently, judgin' by the brogue. When'd
you get here?" His hands busy as he spoke, Tony
pulled a pair of bottled Buds from the ice-packed
bin before him and pried off the caps.

"Last night," Rory replied. "And what a beautiful city it is. So peaceful and prosperous."

Tony set a couple of chilled glasses alongside the
bottles on the bar and looked to Tom like Rory
might have a loose screw. "Did he say peaceful?
Where the fuck's he from? Belfast?"

Before either Rory or O'Meara could reply, a
burly man who'd been eavesdropping on the con-

versation ambled over and clapped a hand on Tom's shoulder. "I hear your friend say he's visiting you, sir? I'm an immigration officer. Could I see his passport and visa?"

O'Meara saw Rory tense, and couldn't contain the broad grin that broke out from ear to ear. "He's busting your balls. Relax. Meet Johnny Velardi, our neighbor, next door to the right. And don't listen to any of his immigrant bullshit. He's one, too. Came over from Brooklyn."

"Brooklyn born and Brooklyn proud," the burly man told Devaney as he shook hands. "It's just soreheaded micks like my neighbor Tom here who call the Verrazano-Narrows Bridge the Guinea Gangplank. Me and mine call it Manifest Destiny."

Rory was clearly lost, and O'Meara moved to shed more light. "Thirty years ago, there was a bare, manageable handful of wops here, and then the city went and built that fucking bridge. Now they think they own the fucking place."

"It's called westward expansion, Sarge," somebody called out from further down the bar.

"It's called infestation," Tom quipped back.

This was clearly a ritual, and other patrons warmed to it as well. From alongside the pool table, across the bar, a short, banty-rooster of a man with slicked-back black hair brandished a pool cue. "Hey, Sarge. Your mick pal know what we call one of these in New York? An Italian hard-on."

"That why y' all have them in your hands, playin' wit' them?" Rory called back.

Gales of laughter erupted from the knot of guys picking parlay bets, and hoots of derision rose from a group of women at one of the booths.

"Good one, Irish!" a heavyset blond woman hollered. "Touché!"

Suddenly, Rory Devaney was enjoying himself. All the tension he'd carried into the place had melted away.

"What's your name, Irish?" Johnny Velardi asked him, hand clapped on his shoulder now.

"Rory Devaney. Pleased t' meet you."

"Pleasure's mine. You hear the one about the Irish lad in Londonderry, tried t' blow up a car? Poor bastard burnt his lips on the fuckin' tailpipe."

Johnny roared with laughter at his own joke, slapping the bar rail, and told Tony he wanted to buy the sarge and his mick friend another round. O'Meara figured they were in for the duration and asked the barkeep to put that gallon jug of milk in the cooler.

"Y' bein' a man of the world, Johnny," Rory addressed his new friend, "I do suppose y' know how t' get ten Italians in a phone box?"

Johnny scowled good-naturedly. "Can't say as I do, Irish. You tell me."

"Y' make one a boss and watch the other nine crawl up his arse."

Johnny Velardi couldn't help it. He laughed almost as hard as he had at his own joke. "So tell me, Rory Devaney," he asked at length. "You play pool?"

Rory glanced over at the table. "Looks t' be a game similar to our snooker. I've played that a time or two. Sure."

"Watchit, Johnny," someone hollered. "He's hustlin' you. Them fuckin' snooker tables over there got pockets so tight the balls squeak goin' in."

Johnny ignored the warning. He indicated the weaselly little guy with the slicked-back hair, and then Tom O'Meara. "Care to place a small wager on a game, Irish? Teams. Me and Bobby Longo there against you and Sarge."

Rory turned to Tom. "You play?"

O'Meara nodded. "I can hold my own."

"Pull out now, like your daddy should o', Johnny," another patron yelled.

"Nine ball. Twenty bucks?" Velardi asked.

When O'Meara reached for his wallet, Rory stopped him. "Let me do this one, Tom. Please. It'll be my pleasure."

For ten tortuous minutes, Johnny Velardi and Bobby Longo looked on as Rory Devaney sank two balls on the break, then proceeded to methodically clear the table. All was quiet in the room until half-way through that run, when somebody in the crowd murmured, "Jesus H." When the last ball dropped, Rory calmly placed his cue on the felt and returned to the bar to fetch his beer. Tom collected their twenty from Johnny.

"Your friend was right," the Irishman told Velardi. "The pockets of our snooker tables are a wee bit tighter than these."

Johnny eyed him warily. "Tom put you up t' this, didn't he? Just t' get my goat."

Rory shrugged. "Never mentioned Tiny's even had a table. But then I never mentioned t' him that I play. A little. Now and then."

Two hours and half a dozen beers later, Tom and Rory tiptoed into O'Meara's house, trying not to make noise. Halfway across the living room, Rory pulled up short.

"Bollocks," he hissed. "We forgot the milk."

"Shit."

"No problem, Tom. I'll run back and get it."

"Hell, it was my responsibility," Tom grumbled, kicking himself. "I'll do it."

"Nonsense, I can see the way that right knee o' yours has been botherin' y'. Go on upstairs."

Upstairs, O'Meara found Sheila propped up in bed reading.

"Hi, babe," he greeted her. "We got a little side-tracked."

"Tiny's?"

"A two-hour trip to the store for a gallon of milk? How'd you guess?"

"You forgot, and left the milk there. Right?"

There were times when he believed this woman could read his mind. "Rory ran back to get it."

"I know. I heard the door. You're limping again, Tom. I noticed it when you came home tonight, and it seems worse now."

"Yeah. Tweaked my knee chasing some mutt kid

this afternoon. Not running. Just getting out of the fucking car."

She closed her book and set it aside, then removed her reading glasses. They were new, something she'd been forced to go to in the past year. She said she hated how old they made her look, but he thought they were cute. Heck, he'd been wearing reading specs for over ten years.

"I'm starting to make good money at what I'm doing, honey," she said. "Maybe it's time. No matter how much you like it, you can't run with the young bucks anymore. Don't make them drag you off the street kicking and screaming. It's undignified."

He began to unbutton his shirt. "Being a good street cop is the only thing I know, Sheel. And the knee's really not all that bad. The orthopedist I saw? He said with arthroscopy, there's a chance he can make it good as new."

She stuffed her glasses into their case, then reached beneath the bedclothes to grab the hem of her nightshirt. Wriggling for a moment, she finally whisked it off over her head. O'Meara felt that characteristic stirring in his loins as he watched her, knowing exactly what she had in mind. After she'd had Annie, it wasn't three months before she had her figure back, working forty-five minutes a day on her NordicTrack machine. She hadn't broken that routine over the six years since, and was in better shape now than she'd ever been in her life. It was something about which she took understandable pride.

"Come to bed, lover," she growled. "We'll talk more about this, later."

As O'Meara slipped out of his jeans, he was glad he'd only had a six-pack, and had called it a night when he had.

8

◆

That Saturday, Rory announced to the O'Mearas that he was taking a trip to Manhattan to see the sights. For the past four days he'd done nothing but travel back and forth to work, he told them, and now his curiosity had reached fever pitch. The lads on the job knew little or nothing about Manhattan sightseeing, but he had purchased himself a detailed map. He'd located St. Patrick's Cathedral, on Fifth Avenue not far from the Rockefeller Center skating rink and the Museum of Modern Art. He'd dreamed for years of taking a ride to the top of the Empire State Building and, by God, he intended to do so. It was a bright, clear autumn day and he ought to be able to see for miles. Tom had advised him that Manhattan was a lot bigger than it looked on a map. Maybe he wanted to try and do this a wee bit at a time, rather than attempt to take the whole apple at once. It sounded like sage advice, and Rory promised to pace himself.

Just to have a story or two to tell, Devaney took that elevator ride to the top of the Empire State Building, where the view was even more spectacular than he'd imagined. Afterward, he wandered up Fifth Avenue, peering in shop and department store windows until he reached St. Paddy's. Inside he skipped the lines outside the confessionals, but did say a quick prayer. For fifteen minutes or so, he watched an Oriental lass with beautiful, shapely legs do jumps, spins, and looping figure eights around the Rock Center rink. Then it was time to get down to the real business at hand.

Burke's Bar, he'd been told, was located in a once scruffy area of Manhattan's West Side called Hell's Kitchen. In recent years, much of that old waterfront and Irish tenement area had been gentrified. To Rory's eye, accustomed to the burned-out streets of Belfast's Catholic ghetto neighborhoods, it looked like Xanadu by comparison. The Tenth Avenue sidewalk outside Burke's was swept clean. The Puerto Rican bodega next door looked prosperous, as did the Moroccan restaurant around the corner. Burke's was the only establishment in evidence that might indicate this had once been an Irish-immigrant enclave. That fabled Irish organized crime outfit, The Westies, was now a rough-and-tumble gang of street thugs from Hell's Kitchen, in name only.

A woman who was obviously a hooker studied

Devaney as he entered the place. He climbed onto a
bar stool, nodded to her in the beveled, back-bar
mirror, then looked away to study the barroom interior. Between the white-and-black-tiled floor and
the ornate, stamped tin ceiling, everything was mahogany. Dark with age, oiled to a gleaming luster,
and lovingly crafted with a plethora of shop-fitted
detail. Wainscotting, heavy, grooved pilasters from
floor to ceiling, and lots of massive crown moldings.
All of the glass in the place, and there was plenty,
had beveled edges and was etched with shamrocks.
There were tables for patrons arranged along a wall
parallel with the bar, and a dining room with white
tablecloths in back. Nice. It told Rory something
about the man he would be dealing with; said he
might well live up to his reputation.

"How you doin' today, honey," the whore's syr-
upy voice crooned in his ear. She'd climbed down
off her stool to saunter over. Rory saw her approach
but ignored it.

"Just fine, Love. Fine and disinterested just the
same. Ta." He fed her a tight-lipped smile that said
fuck off as courteously as he knew how. A pro, she
got the hint, smirked back and wandered away. The
only two other patrons at the bar had watched the
exchange, lost interest, and returned to their drinks.

A slender, ginger-haired barkeep in black bow tie
and dark green apron approached. "What'll it be,
sir?"

Rory nodded toward a pump handle down the
way. "I see y've got stout. A pint, if you please."

"You bet. You from the north?"

"Almost. Ravensdale, in County Louth. Not far from the border a'tall."

When it came to pouring stout, the man knew his business. In no hurry, he filled the glass halfway, let it settle a moment, then filled it a little bit more. "Roscommon," he said as he waited. "Came here with my parents at the ripe age of three. Don't recall much of the old sod. Not from then, anyway."

"Y've been back since, I take it?"

The barkeep ran more Guinness into the glass as he nodded. "Mom moved back home once my dad died. Over ten years ago. I look in on her now when I can."

Rory grunted. "Bloody expensive, a commute like that."

The man smiled and carried the glass to him. "Tell me about it. Thank God Dad did okay while he lived here. That takes a bit of the hurt away."

"What did he do?" Rory wondered. "Your da."

"Poured concrete. Not glamorous, but something everybody seems to need."

It was five minutes later that a fit, prosperous-looking man emerged from the dining room in shirt-sleeves and slacks, followed by a sinister young tough with greasy blond hair in a ponytail. The way that first man moved said he was the proprietor here. He had the confident air of ownership, and when he grabbed the prostitute's ass, any lingering doubts disappeared. She didn't so much as flinch, which said he owned her, too.

Without being asked, the barkeep poured several fingers of Black Bush Irish Whisky over ice and pushed the glass toward the man. Prot whisky, Rory thought. But who was he to talk? Here he was, drinking Prot stout. He continued to sip at it while he studied William Burke in the mirror. Each time Burke started to look his way, he averted his eyes. The moment was Rory's to choose, not the other man's. Another of the big boy's rules.

If anything, Burke seemed to be killing some slow time on a Saturday. He kidded a little with those other two patrons, asked his bartender for a copy of the *Daily News* beneath the bar, and eventually took his drink and his stooge back through the dining room again. Rory finished his stout, then followed.

A staircase marked "private" led from a short hall beside the kitchen door to an open landing one flight up. Rory climbed those stairs to spot Burke and the tough guy in an office, the door left ajar. Burke occupied an expensive leather executive's chair behind a massive old rosewood desk. The other man lounged on a leather sofa.

The tough guy spotted Rory's shadow first and jumped quickly to his feet as Devaney stopped in the doorway. "John's downstairs, pal."

"I'm collectin' for Irish Relief," Rory replied.

"This some kinda fuckin' joke?" The ponytailed man took a step forward as he asked it.

Devaney stood his ground. "No joke, mate."

"Easy, Teddy. It's okay," Burke soothed his

Cerberus. He stood as he spoke and moved around
the edge of his desk, smiling. "The Irish Relief.
That makes you McDuff's man. Pleased to meet
you." He extended his hand. "Billy Burke."

"Pleased t' meet y', Mr. Burke. Rory Devaney."
As he shook hands, Devaney kept his expression
more neutral than the smiling Billy Burke's.

"A good man, Martin McDuff," Burke said.
"And a tough one. But I expect you know that even
better than I." Behind that smile, the tavern owner
was measuring Rory, trying to determine who he
was and the stuff he was made of. Devaney's expression told him nothing. When he didn't bother to
reply, Burke turned and indicated the sofa. "Have a
seat, Mr. Devaney. Make yourself comfortable.
How do you like America?"

Rory strode past Teddy without making eye contact, tossed aside the copy of *Playboy* that the goon
had been ogling, and sat. "I like it fine. The land of
opportunists."

Burke chuckled as he headed back to his desk
chair. "That it is. Look around you. At fourteen I
had a job sweeping up here. Now I own the place,
and three more just like it."

Devaney stared straight at him. "Congratulations,
Mr. Burke. It appears y've done well for yourself."

"And well by you lads, too," Burke reminded
him. "For over twenty years, your lot have not had
a better friend in America than Billy Burke. Not
here, not in Boston, nor any other city you care to
name."

Quite full of himself, this one was. Rory had to sit hard on the urge to yawn. "Once the troubles are ended, I'm sure Belfast will elect some fitting tribute. A statue, perhaps, of St. Billy Burke." That smile he'd grown tired of so quickly, hardened a bit at the edges. Much better. "So, Mr. Burke. When can we take possession of the goods?"

Now Burke eased back in his chair, glanced at Tough Guy Teddy, and grunted. "Possession, you say? These aren't egg rolls you've ordered, friend. AKs or M-16s I could get you in a day. Grenade launchers might take a week. But Stingers? We're talking round the horn from Afghanistan, via Borneo."

"When?" Rory asked again.

Burke shrugged. "Six weeks, minimum. Maybe longer."

Rory thought about the progress he and Sean still needed to make on the boat. They couldn't run the big diesel until the tug was back in the water. There was no telling what sort of problems they might encounter once they did, despite all of Sean's cocky confidence. It was possible they might need all of that six weeks. "How much longer?" he asked.

"Eight weeks, tops. There's no reason it should take more than that."

Rory nodded. "I expect I can use the time profitably, here in the land of opportunists." He let himself smile as he looked directly at Teddy. "You never know. I get lucky, by the time I'm done here, perhaps I'll have bought a goon or two for myself.

Think how impressed all the girls would be, back home."

Burke's smile was back to full wattage. "I'm sure they're plenty impressed already. You got a situation here, or can I help with that? I'd be happy to."

"I'm all sorted out. Thanks."

"Wonderful. Where you staying?"

"I've got friends across the river."

Burke couldn't help himself. He was looking for a handle and hadn't yet found one. Some people refused to be brushed off. "East River or Hudson?"

Rory smiled again. "Take your pick. I'm sure there's nice places t' stay, t' other side of either one."

Burke unfolded his manicured hands from his lap and placed the palms down on the edge of his desk. "O-o-okay. How do I get in touch?"

Rory reached into the pocket of his pants, extracted a piece of paper and handed it across. "Y' call it, ask for Sean."

Burke unfolded the paper and glanced at the number. "Two-one-two is Manhattan."

Devaney held Burke's gaze and nodded. "So it is." He rose slowly to stand face-to-face with the taller and bulkier Teddy. "Y' never introduced me to your guard dog here." He held out his hand to the man. "Rory Devaney, Teddy. Nice t' make your acquaintance."

Teddy glanced down at the hand without taking it, and looked back at Rory to glower.

"There's still the small matter of payment," Burke interrupted them.

Rory turned back to him. "The deal is cash on delivery, Mr. Burke. You knew that."

Burke stood. "Have a nice day, Rory Devaney. Or whoever you are. You Belfast boys all born such hard-ons, or is it something you grow into?"

Rory smirked and started for the door. "Just us ones who survive, Mr. Burke. Ta for now."

9

It was fifteen years since Frankie McGuire said good-bye to his mother in the garden outside their seaside Carnlough cottage and went off to Belfast to fight the Orangemen with the Provisional Irish Republican Army. Within two years it had become unsafe for him to return home to visit his ma and sister. On a handful of occasions in the years since, they'd each traveled to Dublin in the south to meet for precious little time. The government in the south had agreed to help the British apprehend so-called terrorists, and Frankie McGuire was a wanted man all over the globe. During the time of his virtual exile in his own native land, Frankie had all but forgotten what family life could be about.

As Rory Devaney, he'd been apprehensive about staying with anyone who had no sympathy, other than passing, for his cause. For years, he'd held America, and the soft pampered life its citizens led, in scorn. What could any of them know about the troubles, unless they experienced them firsthand? What did any of them know about comrades fallen to British and UVF bullets? Even the most ardent Boston barroom drunk knew nothing of the real hatred that ran in Rory's veins.

Perhaps it had started to happen as early as that first evening when he and Tom O'Meara went out for milk together. In the course of annihilating those Italians at the pool table, he'd let his guard down, let himself empathize with who Tom was and the life he lived. The next thing he knew, the man had started to grow on him. So had his family, in the two weeks that followed. Little Annie was a bright, shining jewel. Morgan, in the throes of puberty and riding a tide of surging hormones, was a bundle of confused emotions that bobbed like a cork on a tempest-tossed sea. Up and down. Never in her control. Bridget was another sort of contradiction altogether. She had all of life figured out and it was her proud, superior secret. So why, he might have asked her but never would, did she suffer such strong misgivings about what others thought of her? Why did she care so desperately? Not about what her family thought, of course, but her school chums and strangers on the street. Boys especially. Oh yes, boys.

And as much as he'd become unexpectedly fond of Tom O'Meara, Rory had also fallen just a bit in love with his wife, Sheila Molloy O'Meara. She was crazy about her man, crazy about her kids, crazy about the success she'd met in her new career: a woman in love with life. True, she'd met with little or no adversity of consequence, but who was Rory to begrudge her, or any of them, their good fortune?

The occasion was another Saturday. The weather had turned unusually warm for November, a phenomenon referred to by everyone who commented on it as "Indian Summer." On Wednesday, little Annie had proposed a family picnic at nearby Tottenville Beach Park, and by Friday night, as the weather held, she was beside herself with enthusiasm for the project. There was no question about whether Rory would attend or what his duties would be. He was going to build a fire and help roast weenies. After they ate, he would assist Annie in the construction of some special dessert called S'mores. And at some juncture he would try to teach Annie how he did that neat "bouncy thing" with a soccer ball atop his foot.

With midday temperatures loitering in the low seventies, Rory was astonished to see how deserted the beach park was. In Ireland, any day that the mercury climbed to such lofty heights as this, citizens would swarm the shoreline in hordes. But then this was a different world, where the people were spoiled by long, dependably warm summers.

"I'm afraid we're creatures of habit," Sheila explained as Rory sat tending his fire. "Come Labor Day and the start of school, the beach season pretty much ends."

"Labor Day. As opposed to Tory Day?" he wondered.

She laughed that gay, infectious laugh of hers. "No, no. As in a day to celebrate the accomplishments of organized labor. At least that was the original intention. Now it's sort of a holiday to pat everybody with a job on the back."

"And to mark the end of summer."

"That's probably even more to the point now, I suppose. We've lost track of most of the reasons we do things."

He thought about that, and realized that Americans weren't alone there. Most people probably had.

"Do you think you can teach Annie that trick with the ball?" she asked. "She's become obsessed."

"It took me years of practice t' get any good at it, but surely I can get her started. Off on the right foot, so t' speak."

Across the grass, Tom and Annie had one of those colorful, acrobatic kites run out to the end of its tether while Bridget flew another one of her own. The wind wasn't really stiff enough to make them as agile as they were designed to be, but none of them seemed to care much. They were playing. Having fun. As Rory watched them, he wondered when he'd last had any real fun. That night on the pool table with Tom and the Italians was as close as he'd let himself get in years. He hated to admit how good it had felt. But fun was nothing he could let himself dwell on.

"What about women, Rory?" Sheila asked out of the blue. "Good-looking man like you should have them flocking, eating out of your hand." She started to say something else, stopped herself, and colored.

"What?" Rory demanded.

"It never even occurred to me that . . ." she paused, then rushed on. "And it's none of my business, of course. I'm sorry. I shouldn't pry."

It evoked a quick, sharp bark of laughter. "Me? Y' wonder if maybe I'm a poof? Ah, no, Sheila O'Meara. I'm a rabid heterosexual who's been on his best behavior. I'm glad Judge Fitzsimmons didn't tell y'."

She frowned, puzzled. "Tell us what?"

"That in Belfast, when mothers hear I'm in their neighborhood, they lock up their daughters." He said it with a merry twinkle in his eye.

She raised her gaze skyward and shook her head. "I'd laugh if I didn't fear it might be true. And if all three of my own girls didn't have crushes on you."

And I, a wee bit of one on you, too, Mrs. O'Meara, he thought. "Once your Annie turns eighteen, you might have reason to worry," he warned her. "That child is an angel."

"So was Bridget at that age, and Morgan, too. Sometimes I wish you could freeze them. At six, they're little pieces of perfection."

"Little girls, perhaps. I was a hellion at her age, m'self."

She gave him a sly, appraising look. "I bet you were, at that. But what good is any man without a little hellion in him?"

Rory grunted and reached to prod his fire. If she only knew the half of it. "I'd say these coals are about ready for weenies."

In a basement office at Whitehall, in London, Harry Sloan faced an assembly comprised of one regular army major general, the SAS brigadier who'd accompanied him during that failed action in Belfast last summer, the United States Embassy's FBI liaison, another man from their Department of State, and various of his MI5 superiors.

"We have information developed through German Interpol sources that McGuire probably spent as many as three weeks in the Frankfurt radical Maoist underground. We still don't know which route he took to get there, but suspect it was via Libya."

"We're more concerned with where he went from there," SAS brigadier Morris complained. "You've been trying to secure a line on him since August, Sloan. This is all you can tell us?"

One of Sloan's Five-Section superiors intervened for him. "Be patient, Arthur. He's getting to that."

"Patient?!" Morris snarled. "You didn't lose eight good men to that infernal bastard. The Major General and I did. All following intelligence Sloan here developed."

"Their security is better than we believed," Harry admitted. "But it may have sprung a tiny leak. Only time will tell. I'll let Mr. Fred Humphries from the Federal Bureau of Investigation tell you a bit more about it."

All eyes turned to the bullet-headed American in the ill-fitting suit. Of course, considering the thick, weight lifter's neck, massive shoulders, and barrel chest, there was some question of whether any suit of clothes would look normal on this man. Even the best of tailors would be challenged.

"For the past eight years, ever since the Soviet Army withdrew from the Afghanistan conflict, we and our CIA have been busy trying to learn the whereabouts of unaccounted-for Stinger missiles supplied clandestinely by our government to the Afghani Mujahedeen," he told them, and paused to let the implications sink in. "Our estimates are that as many as three hundred of those shoulder-fired surface-to-air weapons may have gone unused. Thus far we've been able to track down and take one hundred twelve of them out of circulation. Upward of two hundred still remain at large."

Sloan assumed that this was not news to anyone in that room. Humphries was only laying the groundwork for what he would say next.

"Last week," the FBI man continued, "one of our moles, planted deep in the black-market weapons trade, heard two concurrent rumors. One involved a shipment of forty Stinger missiles from an Islamic arms dealer in Indonesia to an unknown buyer somewhere on America's eastern seaboard. The other rumor is that Frankie McGuire is hiding somewhere in the U.S. Northeast, waiting to take possession of a shipment of ordnance, possibly missiles, that the IRA has purchased."

"And, clever fellows that you are," Brigadier Morris concluded. "You've put two and two together."

The bullet-headed Humphries eyed him steadily. "You know this McGuire's rep better than we do, Brigadier. Wouldn't you?"

Rory and Sean were so eager to take advantage of the warm turn in the weather that they'd worked like animals scraping and sandblasting their tug's hull the week before the O'Meara family's picnic at the beach. That Friday, they'd sprayed on heavy coats of white and barnacle-resistant red paint. Weekend drying conditions proved perfect, and when both men arrived at the Tottenville boatyard Monday morning, their once dilapidated watercraft was a thing to behold.

"And y' thought she was shit, ready for the scrapyard torch," Sean chided his mate. "Look at her, Fr . . . Rory. In't she beautiful?"

"Aye," Rory had to admit. "She is that." The ache in his muscles from all that backbreaking manual labor had subsided enough so he was able to crawl from bed without pain that morning. He touched her starboard flank with a finger to test the tack of the epoxy paint and found it bone dry. "Now to make arrangements t' have her put back in the water. That diesel seizes up when we start her, we've still got an Everest t' climb before we're headed home."

"I'm tellin' y' it'll run like a top," Sean chided.

"But we still ain't goin' nowhere, not into the drink, not anywhere else, either, 'til we pull that prop and swap it."

Rory surveyed the wrecked prop, over four feet across and weighing better than a ton, and then looked to the salvaged one delivered there by truck that past Thursday. The yardmaster had a six-ton Hyster forklift he said they could rig chains to use to lift the old prop out of place and the new one back in. No mean feat, even so.

"Well, I don't know what we're waitin' for," Devaney said. "A snowstorm, perhaps, t' bury this rig arse deep until April?"

Sean grinned and returned to his car to remove something from the backseat. "I thought we'd do this first." With a flourish, he removed a rubber band from a roll of waxy paper and told Rory to hold one end. Slowly, he walked backward to reveal a parade of block letters, each of them eighteen inches high. "Her papers say she was christened *Voyager* at her launch in 1958. Name's been changed a half-dozen times since, but I think that first one's appropriate. You?"

"Aye," Devaney replied. " 'Tis a fine name, indeed." He fingered one of the letters. The final *R*. "Feels like plastic."

"A special sort o' vinyl. Y' transfer it t' the painted surface wit' a heat gun. As it gets hot, it bonds t' the paint. This one's for her stern. I've got two more in the car, one for either side of her bow."

*   *   *

After supper that Monday night, an exhausted Rory Devaney wanted nothing more than to crawl between the sheets and sleep for ten hours. Tom announced he was headed off to Tiny's to watch a football game between the Giants and Washington Redskins and wondered if Rory wanted to tag along. The Irishman begged off, knowing how late those Monday night games went, and how much he needed his rest. Sheila had a house to show a pair of Italian newlyweds from Brooklyn, and figured she'd be gone for several hours. Annie was put to bed at eight-thirty, the obligatory bedtime story told, before Tom could go off to the bar. Sheila left the house at the same time he did, and Rory started for the basement stairs, visions of sugarplums dancing.

"Rory," Morgan hailed him from the floor above. "Bridget's got the new Counting Crows, but she's too stuck-up to ask if we can listen to it on the good stereo in Daddy's bar."

Devaney's heart sank.

"I am not, you twerp," Bridget yelled at her sister from further down the upstairs hall.

"She's got a crush on you," Morgan whispered knowingly. "Thinks you're the hunkiest guy she's ever seen. I heard her tell Holly on the phone last night."

"I'm gonna kill you!" Bridget screamed.

"If Annie's not awake already, she will be soon," Rory warned them. "Come down and use the stereo if y' please. I wouldn't mind hearin' the new Countin' Crows m'self." Under the present circumstances, this was a lie, of course. He thought Adam Duritz a wonderful songwriter and the Crows a fine band, but he'd wrestled a three-thousand-pound prop off his boat that afternoon, and had another to mount, come morning. The forecast called for cold rain and high winds on Wednesday. They needed to have their exterior labors concluded by then.

A sullen Bridget appeared at the head of the stairs, beaming hatred at her sister. "Well, if you don't mind, you being our guest and all, it would sound pretty cool, turned up." She lifted her chin and held her head high to meet his eye as she spoke. "But what she said about me having a crush on you? That's bullshit. You're pretty good-looking, but you're almost old enough to be my dad." There was challenge in her look. She was daring him to contradict her, but he wasn't about to bite. Seventeen years young or not, she was appealing to the animal side of his nature, and he'd been too long without any kind of female company.

"Go on, girl," he replied. "Play your new CD. But please. Not loud enough t' wake your little sister."

A look of confusion spread across her face as Rory started down the hall toward the living room. "Where are you going? I thought you wanted to listen, too."

"Some other time, perhaps. I'm an old man, remember? Until you're done, I think I'll stretch out on the sofa."

When a gentle hand shook Devaney awake, he had no idea how long he'd been sleeping. He opened his eyes to see Sheila O'Meara peering down at him, a look of concern on her face.

"You looked so peaceful, I wasn't sure I should wake you," she told him. "But a bed would be so much more comfortable. Is everything all right?"

"Oh fine," he said, yawning and stretching a crick from his neck. "The girls had a new CD they wanted to play on their da's grand big stereo. I couldn't begrudge 'em that."

"If I was as tired as you looked at dinner, I could have. No problem."

He smiled, "It's your house. Besides, you're their mother. How did your appointment go?"

As she shrugged out of her coat and crossed the room to hang it, he admired the strong, straight line of her back. "They loved the house but aren't sure they can afford it. They're going to talk to their parents. See what sort of help they can give them."

"It's remarkable t' me that their parents would be able to give any help at all," he said. "Where I come from, the thought would never occur to anyone I knew. Nor, I suppose, would the notion of most newlyweds buyin' a house."

She hooked the hanger on the pole and closed the closet door, then turned to face him. "Both my sets of grandparents were born in Ireland. But still, I can't imagine the sort of world you come from, Rory."

"You're lucky . . . to've not witnessed the cruelty, Sheila. It would tear your heart out t' know another mother like yourself; one who's lost a baby t' some Brit bastard's bullet. I've seen the grief with my own eyes. I can see it even now when I close them."

Thoughtful, she remained where she stood, arms crossing to hug herself. And then she shivered, no doubt thinking of how it would feel to lose little Annie, or any of her girls, to tragedy. "All because of religion."

Rory sat up and yawned again. "Nay," he countered. "Religion's just the cheapest and easiest explanation. It's because one day, a long time ago, one man thought it was his right to step on another man's neck. And for too long, that other man let him."

It made Rory a bit uncomfortable to have Sheila O'Meara regard him the way she did. It was clear that she'd seen him in a different light for the first time, and was moved by what she saw.

"It's sad in a way," she said.

"How is that?"

"That any man should have to be so wise beyond his years as you've become. It's the same thing I saw in Tom when we first met. Six years spent working the streets had made him different than other guys I knew."

Rory smiled. "I think y' love him very much. Whoever his job has made him."

Her smile matched his own. "I'm nuts about him. How many women married twenty-three years can say that?" She uncrossed her arms, breathed deep, and sighed. "I feel about as tired as you looked at dinner. Think I'll turn in. How's that job, by the way? It seems like they're working you pretty hard."

He heaved himself to his feet, ready to take possession of his basement domain once again. "What is it you call a man who's drawn my lot? The low man on the totem pole, I think? I'm that, even among us laborers. And laborer is a fairly descriptive term."

Sean Geary was late getting to work at the boatyard the next morning. When he drove up at close to ten o'clock, he wore the smug look of a well-fed sexual predator. Rory had arrived at the work site two hours earlier and, single-handed, rigged chains to hoist their new propeller with the boatyard's Hyster forklift.

"Well, look who's decided t' grace me with his presence," Devaney growled. "Where the fook you been? As if I couldn't hazard a guess. Y' heard a different weather forecast than me, Sean?"

Geary ignored the barbs in his partner's words as he stepped close to inspect Rory's progress. "Y' need t' get yourself laid, mate," he murmured. "T'ain't healthy, keepin' all that urge t' have it off bottled up inside y' for so long as you have." He reached to grab hold of one taut chain and gave it a fierce jerk. When it held fast, he nodded with satisfaction. "Why don't you run the lift while I guide her."

Rather than move toward the Hyster, Rory stood where he was. "When, where, and who I choose t' fook ain't none o' your goddam business, Sean Geary. When y' choose t' show up for work is plenty of mine. Burke calls and this fookin' tub isn't ready, we got a whole other headache t' deal with."

Sean refused to take up the challenge in Rory's words. In a loose but technically important sense, Frankie McGuire, aka Rory Devaney, was Geary's commanding officer. Sean preferred to let the emphasis fall on *loose*. He shrugged Rory's rebuke off the same way he always did, with a smirk and easy wave of the hand. "Speakin' o' Burke. He called. Said he needs t' see you."

Damn your eyes, Sean Geary, Rory thought. "When?" he demanded impatiently.

"No more'n an hour ago. I was busy tryin' t' get my Colleen o' the moment t' shift arse. He calls and says just what I told y'. Called me Sean and asked my last name, too. I told 'im t' quit wit' the comedy routine."

Rory thought back to his meeting with Burke in the office at the arms merchant's tavern. Information was power, and it was a power game that Billy Burke played. But, for a man with alleged sympathies for the Provisional IRA's cause, Burke wanted to know too damned much. "See me when?" he asked.

"I took the liberty o' tellin' him you're gonna be kind of tied up t'day. He sounds like a man likes t' call the shots. Didn't like bein' told y' wouldn't exactly come runnin'."

"I asked when, Sean." A cold wind cut across the Arthur Kill waterway from out of the northwest, pushing a band of cirrus clouds high overhead. Those clouds seemed to confirm the forecasted precipitation, sometime later that night. The only question in Devaney's mind was what form that precipitation might take.

"I figure, once we get the boat in the water, I'll need at least a day wit' the engine, even after we determine if it'll run. It's s'posed t' squall anyway. I told Burke you'd be callin' round t' his place, sometime in the mornin'."

Devaney grunted and started for the forklift. "Let's get this bastard in place and secured." He climbed up to take the controls, and paused before starting the Hyster's engine. "What exactly did y' mean, Sean. If it'll run. If I'm not mistaken, y've already assured me she'll run like a top."

Geary grinned and threw him another of his devil-may-care waves of the hand. "I'm a mechanic, mate, not the fookin' Pope. Y' want infallibility, call the Vatican."

The yardmaster was clearly impressed with the job the two young Irishmen had done on that wreck of a tug left littering his landscape for the past fifteen years. He was equally impressed with the forethought they'd shown, soaking the mechanism of the long-frozen dry-docking apparatus on which the tug sat. The boat cradle, built on a series of axles and wheels not dissimilar to a boxcar's, broke free when given a good tug from the winch. It rolled forward along its rails with an anguished scream of protest, and then, as oil-soaked rust dislodged, and wheels ran free, that scream became a low, moaning wail. By the time the bow of the craft kissed water, the only noise those wheels made was a mere, low rumbling.

Rory, ashore with the yardmaster, watched with weary satisfaction as the lowermost blade of that freshly installed prop took its first taste of saltwater, then slowly sank from view.

"You boys did one helluva job," the yardmaster complimented. He indicated Sean, onboard the tug and intently watching its progress from his position in the stern well. "That buddy of yours surprised me. Hops around like he's got a bug in his fuckin' britches, but get him alongside a diesel engine and he goes all calm and focused. Like a heart surgeon. I told him he ever wants a job, call me first."

Rory knew as much about heart surgery as he did about big diesel engines, but was relieved to hear such high regard expressed for his friend's abilities. No one was more cocky confident than Sean Geary, and nothing came cheaper from most Irishmen than talk. "I think she'll prove seaworthy enough," was all Rory said in reply.

Aboard the *Voyager*, an hour later, Rory Devaney loitered in the cramped little engine room and looked on as Geary stood back from the power plant to wipe his greasy hands on a rag. "She's ready as she'll ever be, mate. Here goes noothin'."

Rory would hardly call what happened next nothing. He was frankly impressed with the diesel's transformation from hulking, grease-begrimed mess to the gleaming machinery that now stood before him. While he'd slaved ondeck to make the cabin, galley, and helm serviceable, Sean had spent hours on end down here, rebirthing his baby. His love for the work showed in the tiny details. Little brass fittings were polished to a high shine. Everything else had been repainted bright red and green. Gauge faces were scrubbed clean, glass replaced where once it was cracked or altogether missing.

"Y' want t' fire it from the helm or down here?" Rory asked.

"After all this work? I've got t' watch it turn over. You can go above and start it from there if y' want. Or I can jump the starter from here."

Still as doubtful as Thomas himself, Rory was tempted to absent himself and head for the helm. But then again, if it did fire and kick over, he wanted to be there to witness it, too. "Go ahead. I'm sittin' on fookin' pins here."

Sean set about snaking a length of cable from a starter-motor terminal to the brand-new marine batteries hooked together in series along one bulkhead. The end for the batteries had a spring clamp attached. He handed that to Rory. "When I say fire, y' touch it to the negative there, until I say quit."

Rory held his end and nodded. Geary busied himself with an aerosol can of ether, opening petcocks and spraying a burst atop each of the dozen cylinder heads. At the number-one cylinder, he held the can poised, crossed the fingers of his free hand, and flashed that what-the-hell grin of his. "Fire."

The instant that Devaney made contact between battery and starter, the big diesel's guts rumbled. When Sean sprayed more ether onto the number-one head, the whole machine suddenly shuddered, coughed, and snarled to life. Geary frantically signaled Rory off the battery terminal, lest he burn out the starter motor, and as Devaney backed away, he watched in amazement as the big rumbling diesel settled down to drone with the deafening racket so typical of these machines.

"Whoa-ho!" Sean whooped, his face seamed ear-to-ear with a grin of smug satisfaction. "Did I tell y', or did I tell y'? Just listen to this fookin' beast!"

Sean had proven himself an accomplished marine mechanic. But big diesels and smaller gasoline-powered engines were as much as he knew about the actual operation of boats. As an apprentice and then a journeyman mechanic in the Belfast shipyards, he'd ridden aboard a variety of vessels during proving runs, but had never taken the helm. It was some years since Rory had last taken a boat out, but over the past week he'd spent several hours each afternoon familiarizing himself with this vessel's bridge controls. At night, he'd pored over charts of those waters immediately off Tottenville and the southernmost tip of Long Island.

Late that afternoon, the *Voyager* and those two obsessed men who proposed to take her three thousand miles across the open North Atlantic, made their first foray into Arthur Kill and the waters of Raritan Bay. Aware of the tug's intended purpose in life, Rory knew he shouldn't be surprised at the vessel's nimble maneuverability. To his boyhood fisherman's eye, she'd looked too squat and ungainly on land. But at sea, her prow rode high and confident in the water, while her aft gunwales and stern sat low and streamlined. Pushed to full power, the wake she threw was impressive. That huge single screw dug hard to send the entire shuddering vessel surging ahead across windswept seas at close to ten knots.

"What d' y' think?" Sean hollered in Devaney's ear against the roar of the engine.

"I think that Portrush is a long fookin' distance off," Rory yelled back. "But she's got a sound feel, this little tug has. We don't hit weather, we just might make a go of it."

10

Just as the Weather Channel had predicted, the Northeast was slammed with a bone-chilling rainstorm that night. Mixed with sleet, the rain came down hard, driven sideways at times by fierce gusts of arctic wind. That evening, Rory Devaney was smart enough to stay home out of the inclement weather, but the next morning when he rose, he found the storm still at full blow. As much as he might have wanted to stay indoors and enjoy the quiet of the house once the girls had all departed for school, he had an appointment to keep with Billy Burke.

Rush hour was long over by the time Devaney hurried half-soaked up the St. George Station access ramp and caught a ferry to Manhattan. Throughout his journey across New York harbor, he couldn't help but wonder how his little tug would fare on the open ocean, in conditions like these. In the waters of the North Channel and beyond, into the North Atlantic, he'd seen swells reach heights of fifteen feet. He knew they could grow to much higher than that, and doubted the *Voyager* would be happy in anything over fifteen feet. He knew for a fact that *he* wouldn't be. Loaded with as much fuel as they intended her to carry, the boat was sure to wallow for the first fifteen hundred miles. Sometimes, in heavy weather, that wasn't a bad thing, as long as they held a course steady into oncoming seas. But once that extra ballast was burned, a twenty-foot swell would toss the craft like a cork. Ah, well. Rory was prepared to leave the worrying to philosophers. He feared he'd gotten soft, this month he'd spent in America.

Burke's was not yet busy with its usual workweek lunch crowd when Rory pushed past the front door and in out of the freezing rain. There was a different bartender on duty today. This one was older, with the pasty, slightly dissipated look of a defrocked Irish priest. A half-dozen patrons loitered on stools at the bar, most of them in suit coats and ties, and keeping to themselves. Ever cautious, Rory had spent a moment on the rainy sidewalk, examining the patrons through the window glass. Now, as he took a stool at the far end of the bar from the dining room entrance, he took another moment to study them again. Two glanced his way as he sat, then returned to their newspaper crosswords and drinks.

None of the rest even bothered to look up. All, save one, looked like salesmen seeking a port in the storm. The last could have been an actor. He sat at a table, legs crossed, a beer at his elbow and what looked like a script in one hand. His lips moved as he read. Reasonably confident that today's cast of characters were not part of some elaborately contrived MI5-FBI trap, Rory relaxed as much as he could, and signaled the barkeep. He ordered a pint of stout.

Though Rory had seen no television monitors in evidence the previous time he'd visited here, he guessed Burke must have some means of watching the bar from his upstairs office. Seated with his stout for perhaps five minutes, he noticed movement in the dining room from the corner of one eye, and looked that way to see Billy and his pet baboon, Teddy, approach at an easy, proprietary gait. Several times along the bar, Burke stopped to say hello to one patron or another, And like it was choreographed, the barkeep scooped ice into a tumbler, poured in a deft two fingers of Black Bush, and set the glass within the boss man's easy reach as he passed.

"Rory Devaney." Billy lifted his glass in toast as he arrived to stand at Rory's side.

Devaney nodded. "Mr. Burke. I understand you called."

Burke flashed a tight, phony smile. "Indeed. Yesterday. Only to be informed you would be otherwise engaged until this morning."

When called upon, Rory could play smarmy as

well as the next man. "I hope it's no great inconvenience to you, sir. If it is, please accept my apologies. I'm afraid I was out of town."

"Ah. I trust you were enjoying yourself?"

Rory smiled. "Immensely. A friend and I went sailing."

Burke clearly couldn't decide whether his left leg or his right was being pulled. Prudently, he moved on. "You like oysters, Rory Devaney?"

"Aye. Indeed I do, sir."

"We just got a fresh shipment of Blue Points this morning. Why don't I have the kitchen shuck you a dozen?"

Suffering Jesus, Rory thought. Billy Burke, patron saint of the Irish resistance, was offerin' him a free lunch. "Ta, but no. I think I'll just have whatever news y've got for me. Then I'll be runnin' along. That train back t' Brooklyn, New Jersey, 's a right bloody pain."

The phony smile faded. "Why do I get the feeling you don't trust me, son?"

"I like t' stay on equal footin' with whomever I'm dealin', sir. I trust y' as much as you trust me."

Perhaps the smile that Burke returned was a bit more genuine than the last, but not by much. "Ah. I'd forgotten. You're the survivor."

"What is it y' wanted t' see me about, Mr. Burke?"

"Your merchandise has arrived."

"Indeed. And it's in your possession?" This was at least two weeks ahead of the earliest projected date, and Rory was more than a bit relieved that the *Voyager*'s power plant ran as soundly as Sean had assured him it would. "I'll want a look, of course. Before payment is made."

"A look." Burke appeared to mull this notion over, and then looked sideways at Devaney. "You're one of those old-fashioned guys, won't fuck until he's married, right?"

"I'm more worried about gettin' fooked than fookin', Mr. Burke. Take me to them blindfolded, you're worried about me trying' t' hijack 'em from y' later."

Now Burke was facing Rory straight on. He kept his eyes riveted, and neither blinked. "Fair enough," he said at length. "Just you?"

"I'll want t' bring along my mechanic," Rory replied. "I wouldn't know an operational Stinger from a martini."

After a call was placed to Judge Pete Fitzsimmons that noon, Rory was asked to stop by the man's Tenth Street town house at six o'clock that evening. Later, he killed time in a lively Greenwich Village bar called the Dew Drop Inn, and called Sheila to say he wouldn't be home for supper that night. He explained that a coworker had invited him to meet friends in an Irish enclave in the North Bronx. He had no idea how late he might get back.

Located a few doors west of Fifth Avenue, on the north side of Tenth Street, the Fitzsimmons residence was one of the more opulent single-family dwellings on that upmarket Greenwich Village block. Constructed of brownstone, with a wide, gated front stoop, it stood four stories tall, with slender, arched windows on the parlor floor. The judge had suggested Devaney ring the bell on a door a few feet below street level, to the right on the stoop. When Rory did so, he was forced to wait nearly five minutes before he heard the approach of footsteps. Irked, he was at least thankful that the earlier rainstorm had passed.

It was hard to be sure, but the maid who answered the door was probably Rory's own age. Thickset and dour, she was heavy on her feet, with the slouched shoulders of one who thought the mere drawing of breath to be a burden. When she spoke it was with the accent of a west-country peasant. "The jooge, he said t' see y' upstairs. Mind y' wipe yer feet. I been all bleedin' day at that floor."

She led the way down a hall past an impressive kitchen and laundry room to a tiny private elevator. Together, they rode in the cramped car to the third floor. All the way, Rory was conscious of the odor of stale sweat on the woman, mixed with the faint stink of alcohol. For some, America hadn't proved the land of opportunists, but just another place to grow old and die.

When Devaney stepped out of the car into a dark paneled room lined with leather-bound volumes, he found the judge seated behind a desk of massive proportion. A merry fire crackled on the grate in the hearth before him, and there was a decanter of whisky on a silver tray. The several tumblers on the tray stood empty, while the one at Fitzsimmons's right elbow was poured nearly half full.

"Come in, Rory lad," the judge greeted him. "Grab any of these chairs you like. Whisky?"

Devaney took a seat in a leather upholstered club chair and nodded. "Aye. Might warm me up. I was a while standin' in the wind on your bloody stoop."

Fitzsimmons filled one of the empty glasses to the top, handed it across, and shrugged philosophically. "You've got to forgive our Margaret. At twenty-two she was struck by lightning. She's never been the same since. Used to be the most cheerful lass you're ever likely to meet."

Once Rory was sure the little elevator was long departed, he reached inside his jacket and withdrew an envelope. "I assume we'll be left alone here?" he asked.

The judge nodded. "My wife has her reading group tonight. The nanny is downstairs on the first floor, with our daughter."

This news surprised Devaney. "Y've got a child, young enough t' need a nanny?" The judge had to be at least sixty.

Apparently, Fitzsimmons was accustomed to such questions. "Juliet is my second wife. My first died of cancer ten years ago. Our daughter is six."

The same age as Annie O'Meara, Rory reflected. He wondered how old that made Juliet, but refrained from prying further. "These are the photographs Burke gave me this mornin' of the merchandise."

He opened the envelope and spread five snapshots on the desk between them as he spoke. "That's yesterday's dateline on each copy of *The New York Times*." He tapped the spot where a copy of the *Times* was draped over a crate full of missiles in one of the shots. "I told him that before we pay, I'll still need t' make visual confirmation. He's agreed I can take Sean along."

"It's one hell of a lot of money," Fitzsimmons mused. He lifted a photograph to study it. "You're confident that Geary can assure us they're operational?"

"That's why he's here, Judge. He's the ordnance expert."

Fitzsimmons lowered the picture to look hard at his visitor. "For three million, cash, he'd better make good and goddamned sure."

Once their meeting was over, rather than send Rory back down to the basement via the elevator, Pete Fitzsimmons led the way to the main staircase. Rory told him he would let him know how it went, as soon as he and Sean returned from their inspection tour the next day. Fitzsimmons assured him that most of the cash was ready now. When the time came to exchange cash for goods, the rest would be in his possession as well.

Halfway down that flight of stairs toward the second-floor landing, the sound of a woman's voice, raised in song, reached Rory's ears. Of startling strength and clarity, it stopped him for a moment.

"Low lie the fields of Athenry," it sang. "Where

once we watched the small free birds fly. Our love was on the wing, we had dreams and song to sing . . ."

As he listened, Rory continued more slowly down the stairs, trying to imagine the source of such a voice. At the second-floor landing, he made the turn to start down that last flight to the front door and saw the top of a small, blond girl's head cradled against the shoulder of a slender woman. They were seated on a stair tred, midway down. One of the singing woman's hands stroked the sleeping child's head, her long, slender fingers gently combing through the child's loose golden locks. The hair on her own head was the rich color of old mahogany. It fell to her shoulders in a thick, wavy mass.

For the long, paralyzed instant it took Rory to force his feet to take the next downward step, he wanted that scene, and the sound of that voice, to freeze in all its crystal clarity. Right there, before he saw her face, and the spell was broken forever.

". . . It's so lonely 'round the fields of Athenry."

His next step caused the stairs to creak. The woman jerked around, startled, her singing cut short. She stared wide-eyed at the stranger who descended toward her, perhaps the most beautiful young woman Rory Devaney *or* Frankie McGuire had ever seen.

"I'm sorry," he murmured in apology as he edged past. "Didn't want t' interrupt your singing. But didn't mean t' startle y' like that, neither."

She smiled while shaking her head. "Pay it no mind," she replied. "I didn't know the judge had company. Be sure t' button up. 'Tis cold as a landlord's heart out there t'night."

Outside the house, Rory stood on the sidewalk below the stoop and looked back toward the door he'd just passed beyond. That was not a woman, but a mirage, he told himself. He'd sailed too long on this empty sea without female companionship. Now he was seeing them on staircases, singing like sirens.

The shadow of movement in an upstairs window caught his eye. He looked up to see Pete Fitzsimmons staring down at him. With a nod, he bade the good judge a last good night, and started on his way.

Tom O'Meara had the four-to-midnight tour that week and thus far that night, things in the upper reaches of Manhattan had been blessedly quiet. On night tours, he let himself off the midday cabbage and carrot routine to eat a regular supper, and tonight he and Eddie Diaz had chosen a Cuban-Chinese joint on 193rd and Broadway. Eddie could get his requisite fried chicken and other servings of artery-clogging grease, while Tom could go low fat with lo mein, or high carbohydrates and vegetable proteins with red beans and rice. Either way, both of them left happy. On this night, as they climbed back into their car and Tom cranked up the heater, he decided to spare Eddie his daily cholesterol lecture. Diaz hadn't complained once that night about not being able to drive, and Tom supposed slack should be cut both ways.

"Unit twelve-oh-seven. Respond to a domestic disturbance in progress, Fifteen-fifty St. Nicholas Avenue, apartment six-C," the dispatcher's voice came to them over their radios. "See the building manager, apartment one-A. Over."

Diaz made a face as he picked up his radio. He thumbed the transmit key. "Twelve-oh-seven. That's a ten-four. We're rolling. Over." He glanced at his boss as O'Meara swung them out from the curb and hit the gas. "Happy days are here again, boss. Wanna lay money on whether she'll press charges?"

"What? I look like I got stupid overnight?" O'Meara growled.

1550 St. Nicholas Avenue was just three blocks south and two east of where they'd eaten dinner. Tom managed to cover the distance in less than two minutes. He was surprised to see an older woman in a floral-print housecoat actually waiting at the building's front door for them. Usually a tenant made a 911 call to report a domestic disturbance, and then hid behind locked doors until the issue was resolved.

"You the manager?" Tom asked the lady as they approached.

"Señora Esparza. *Sí.* It's the two in *seis*-C. They fight, he punch her all the time. I tell them las' week, next time, I call *policía.*"

Eddie told her to go back into her apartment and

wait for them to come back down. "You keep an eye out," he directed. "If another unit arrives, let them in, *pronto*. *Comprende*?"

She nodded that she understood, said her window looked out onto the sidewalk in front, and hurried off toward her door.

The beat-up elevator looked like it had been out of order for years. Accustomed to such situations in the sector they worked, neither O'Meara nor Diaz gave it a second thought. They started for the stairs. Unlike the common areas of many buildings they visited, this stairwell was swept clean. It smelled strongly of a pine-scented cleansing agent. Señora Esparza, despite the odds, was struggling to run a tight ship here.

Outside the door to 6-C, O'Meara glanced skyward for a moment as though seeking guidance from a higher power. He then raised a fist to hammer at the panel. "Police!" he called out.

Silence greeted them from inside the apartment, while up until he knocked, a screaming fight had raged within. Tom hammered at the door again, and this time Eddie called out.

"Policía! Abra la puerta, por favor!"

The knob rattled and turned, and the door was tugged inward by a young girl of nine or ten. She was wide-eyed, her flushed young face streaked with tears.

"Buenas noches," Diaz greeted her. *"¿Dónde está su madre?"*

The little girl turned and started to point to an

open doorway. Suddenly a tiny woman, long hair in a wild tangle, came flying through it to land on the floor at their feet. Directly in her wake followed an enraged man at least twice her size, waving a 9-mm handgun.

"I kill you, you fucking bitch!" the crazed man screamed. And before either cop could react, the gun was aimed square at the middle of Eddie Diaz's face. "Is this the one you fucking, *puta*? I kill him, too! I kill you both!"

Careful not to even twitch, Tom O'Meara cleared his throat. At the noise, the jumpy lunatic with the gun swung it his way.

"You wanna die, too, motherfucker? This bitch, she make me crazy. You think I don't care . . ."

"I thought your beef was with me, *hombre*," Diaz snapped.

It threw the gunman off. He swung his attention back toward Eddie, now torn between targets for his rage. O'Meara anticipated just that reaction and launched. At the moment of impact, the perp's gun was somewhere in midair and aimed at no one. Bad knee and all, Tom had good balance and just the right amount of momentum to really unload on the guy. A double forearm thrust slammed the jerk hard into the wall and knocked the wind out of him. His weapon clattered to the floor, and in one clean move, Tom spun him and shoved him face-first into the peeling plaster. Eddie was right behind him with the cuffs. He was snapping the second bracelet onto the gagging suspect's wrists when Jerry Walker rushed into the apartment.

"You guys okay?" he gasped, panting.

"Sonofabitch threatened to shoot us," Eddie replied. He grinned. But for his shaking knees, he was the picture of calm. "Big macho stud, can beat up a lady half his size, and wave a gun in the faces of two cops."

"Haul him in," O'Meara told Walker. "Where's Ignacio?"

"Where you think? I lost him on the landin', three floors down."

Tom shoved the cuffed suspect Walker's way. "Put him in a holding cell until we get back. Gotta take statements."

The perp had finally managed to suck in a full breath and was gulping air deep now. Jerry grabbed him by the elbow and started him toward the door. Reaching it, he paused to lift his chin toward the woman of the house. She had a nasty knot turning purple below her left eye, and a small cut on her opposite cheek. "She gonna press charges, or you just goin' through the motions?"

O'Meara's knees were shaking, too. "This time, I don't really give a fuck. Asshole pointed a gun at me, and threatened to kill Eddie, too. She may not press charges, but we sure as hell will."

Behind him, Eddie leaned over to pick up that gun. When he jacked back the action, a shell leapt out to fall to the floor. "One in the chamber. Safety off. Close one, Sarge."

Tom could feel his right knee start to throb again. "Fucking guns," he muttered, and slowly shook his head.

11

◆

The place Billy Burke had designated for the
meet was Jones Beach, a long stretch of sand
on the open ocean off the south shore of Long
Island. On that cloudless morning in mid November,
with temperatures loitering in the high twenties,
Rory and Sean rode east along Ocean Parkway.
Running the length of that sand dune island for over
twenty miles, the roadway was virtually empty. Yesterday's storm had scrubbed the air as clean as Rory
remembered the sea air of his childhood to be.

"High summer, they tell me the city folk flock
here by the fookin' millions," Sean told Rory as he
drove. "Hard t' imagine it now, in't it? Last two
miles, we haen't seen a bleedin' soul."

Which suited Devaney just fine. When Burke had
suggested this location, and Rory later located it on

a map, the whole idea looked barmy. It seemed doubtful to him that anywhere just a few miles removed from one of the most densely populated areas on America's eastern seaboard could be this remote and desolate. "I suspect Bad Billy's done this before," he speculated. "He din't strike me as the sort who takes any chance he doesn't need t'. He's another survivor, like you and me."

From the passenger seat of Geary's little Sunbird, Devaney sat with his map spread across his knees and stared out at the boarded-up lifeguard towers, the stretches of empty parking pavement, and the mothballed roadside concession stands. Off across the sand to the south, a Jeep was parked near the high-tide line. Adjacent to it, two men in parkas were surf casting. Rory wondered what it would be like to take a day, or even a morning, off to go fishing. It was fifteen years since he'd last had a hook in the water, and until this moment he hadn't realized how much he missed it. Perhaps, before they set sail for Ireland, he would procure some line and hooks. Sometime during those fourteen days they expected the Atlantic crossing to take, he might find an hour here and there to fish.

"Should be right along here somewhere," he announced. His finger traced the route they followed, toward an *X* he'd marked on the map just past the Jones Beach Marine Theater.

"That must be them, there." Sean nodded ahead to a panel van parked at the edge of the lot, down close to the sand. Two men with fishing gear and a plastic pail stood beside it, watching the road rather than the sea. "You said one o' them's got greasy long blond hair?"

Sure enough, Rory recognized Billy Burke and his shadow goon, Teddy. Out of habit, he straightened in his seat to turn and scan the surrounding terrain in all directions. "Go on past them half a mile or so," he instructed. "Then we'll turn back." The terrain looked clear to him, from what he could see, but he'd never once regretted being cautious, all his soldiering life.

When they finally pulled into that parking lot and alongside Burke and Teddy's van, Devaney read the scowl of impatience on Billy's face and smiled to himself. The arrogant bugger looked cold, which suited him just fine.

"You drove straight past," Burke complained as they exited the Sunbird. "What? We weren't standing out here plain as day, and my directions weren't specific enough for you?"

"Sean O'Malley, meet Billy Burke," Rory introduced his ordnance man. Burke already had the first name. There was no reason he should also have the last.

"Pleasure," Burke replied. And as he took a step forward to shake hands, he studied this new component, added to the equation. "I hope you know your business, Mr. O'Malley, because it's fucking cold out here and I'd like to be on my way. You've handled one o' these babies before, I take it?"

For a prolonged moment, Geary just stared at him

impassively. He then swung his head to nod at the side door of the van. "You're in such a rush, perhaps we'll dispense with the chitchat and look at what y've brought for us, eh?"

Burke stiffened slightly, and shot a quick glare at Devaney. Then, just as quickly, he was all joviality again. The consummate salesman. "Teddy," he ordered his stooge. "Let's show Mr. O'Malley what he came here to see."

As Teddy grabbed the handle and hauled the door back on its track, Burke stepped to the opening with Sean at his side. Like the astute student of treachery and double cross that he was, Devaney hung back several paces, one hand wrapped around the butt of the automatic pistol he carried concealed in his left coat pocket. If Teddy took one wayward step, Rory would shoot him straight through the pocket lining and exterior shell of his coat. No questions asked. If Burke had a problem with that, he'd shoot him, too.

There was one crate inside the cargo area of the van, close to five feet long and eighteen inches square at each end. Burke reached to lift the crate's lid, pushed it to one side, then picked up one of the three shoulder-fired Stinger launchers contained therein.

"Is this a work of art or what?" he asked, turning to display the weapon. "Fucking dick of death if ever I saw one." And as he spoke, one of his gloved hands stroked the shaft of the launch tube.

"May I?" Sean asked. He started to reach for the weapon, but Burke pulled it back.

"Easy, fella. Your pal there said you wanted to see the merchandise. So look. I get cold cash in hand, you can fondle these fuckers all you want." Burke took a step back from Geary, triggered the shoulder stock release to deploy it, then jerked the telescoping launch tube out another foot to its full extension. "Easy as one, two, three, gents. Badabing, badabing, badaboom."

Rory watched Burke lift the launcher and sight along it, one hand wrapped around the trigger grip. "Dick of death. That's very poetic, don't y' think, Sean?"

"Must be Irish," Sean replied. "It's one o' the paltry few gifts God gave us."

Burke tore his attention from his gun sights to smile at them again. This time, there was a demonic twinkle in his eye. "How many small planes you think go down in these parts every year, Teddy?"

"Plenty, boss," the stooge replied. "Bad weather. Rich-guy doctors and dentists with more balls than brains. Nose plantin' them little play toys of theirs all the fuckin' time."

Rory only half-listened to the goon's words. Off to the south, he saw what had caught Billy Burke's attention. Low to the water, a lone single-engine air-craft rigged with pontoon floats flew east toward the more affluent reaches of Long Island.

"Be a tragedy, of course," Burke continued, "If another happened to go down on a crisp, cloudless autumn morning like the one we've got here."

"Engine trouble, most prob'ly," Teddy mur-mured.

Burke shifted his feet slightly, his concentration now locked on that target a half mile distant. "Without a doubt," he crooned. "What other problem would it have?"

"For fuck sake, man!" Sean complained. "You've made your point."

Bad Billy grunted a low, guttural chuckle. "It makes you feel better, think of it this way: The pilot and whoever else is aboard gave their lives for a Free Ireland."

Rory watched Burke's finger find the trigger. "Pull that," he growled, "and they won't be the only ones give their lives for a fookin' Free Ireland."

A frowning Billy Burke looked away from his sights. He found the muzzle of Rory's pistol aimed dead center at the middle of his chest. Slowly, he lowered the launcher. Off on the horizon, the float plane gradually disappeared from view.

"The man is stone fookin' mad," Sean complained to Rory. "A bleedin' lunatic."

Burke disengaged the launch tube extension, collapsed the folding shoulder stock, and tossed the weapon two-handled to his goon. "Hear that, Teddy boy? Sounds t' me like we've got a couple satisfied customers." He turned back to Rory and gestured toward the gun still in his hand. "Relax, Mr. Devaney. I did summer stock in the Berkshires in my youth. Some said I was reasonably good. To this day, I still prefer a dramatic approach."

* * *

Six weeks ago, Megan Desmond was contacted by Martin McDuff through Judge Fitzsimmons and told she was to function as a secondary conduit to Frankie McGuire in New York. The notion had understandably frightened her. No matter whose side he fought on, Frankie the Angel was notorious. A ruthless killer. The last time Megan had laid eyes on him, she was a mere girl of fourteen. Frankie McGuire, at twenty, was already a seasoned veteran of five years' Belfast street warfare. With his long tangled locks of blond hair, a beard that made him look as old as her father, and those intense blue eyes that seemed to look right through a person. He'd seemed bigger than life itself.

Then, last night when she'd heard that creak behind her on the stairs, with little Molly Fitzsimmons cradled against her shoulder, the handsome man she'd seen descend from the judge's library was so different in appearance from the Frankie she remembered that he was all the way to the door before she knew him. He'd stopped on the landing above to listen to her sing, she was sure of it. And as he'd passed, she was also sure he'd returned her smile. With his passing her so unexpectedly, like that, all fear of who the street legends had made him out to be had vanished.

The knapsack she carried felt heavier than Megan Desmond had thought two million dollars would be. But then what did she know of such things; a nanny who earned two hundred tax-free U.S. dollars a week? She knew, as she proceeded toward her meet with McGuire at the Wollman Ice Rink in Central Park, that the judge walked within sight of her, armed and on the lookout for trouble. Once Frankie showed his face, it was agreed that Judge Fitzsimmons would break off and move on to meet his wife for supper. And Megan, once the handoff was made, would find her way home on her own.

The cold in New York was different than that of Belfast. It wasn't as warm as the North Irish night, this time of year, but also not as damp. Back home, the cold of November nights went so deep toward Megan's bones that she thought she might never thaw until spring. Here, she found this crisp, dry cold more tolerable, and now she walked easily through it. Wondering. What was he like? How had the last eight years changed him? Rumor on the stateside IRA grapevine had it that McGuire was the last man to have seen her brother, Dessie, alive. The last to speak to him. She wanted so much to ask Frankie about that, to know how her brother had died.

Megan's instructions were to stand at the west fence that lined the perimeter of the ice rink and wait. She was happy to get that knapsack off her back and wedge it between her boots as she rubbed her shoulders. Her neck would be stiff tomorrow, of that much she was sure. Beyond the fence, the bright-lit rink was jammed with colorfully clad skaters of all ages, sexes, and races. Some were expert, and some so clumsy they were comical.

" 'Tisn't it lovely, how they glide like that, some

of 'em?" an Irish voice murmured behind her. "Like they haven't a care in the world?"

Her breath caught in her throat, and Megan turned. There, behind her and half in shadow, Frankie McGuire stood leaning against the trunk of a leafless tree. In a leather coat, with a muffler wrapped around his neck, he was hatless. "Y' frightened me," she complained.

"Bad habit of mine, sneakin' up on people. Sorry." He dipped his head as he apologized.

Megan breathed deep and squared her sore shoulders, composing herself. "I don't s'pose y' remember me." She stuck out her hand. "Megan Desmond. Y' knew my brother. And met me when I was a mere lass of fourteen."

His blue eyes seemed to twinkle. "Well there's nothin' mere about y' any longer, Megan Desmond." He took the hand lightly, raised it to his lips and barely brushed them across the back of it. "I'm sorry about Dessie. He was a good lad. One of the very best. Nobody should have t' die the way he did."

Her throat gone suddenly tight, Megan swallowed hard. "I was hopin' y' could tell me more about it, Frankie. All I've heard is the rumors. One of them claims you were there."

McGuire eased around her to stand staring through the fence at the skaters. "Aye. I was indeed. We were all caught in a trap. Some traitor tipped the Brits to our new safe house. Dessie was on the roof. Got himself wounded bad in a firefight with two

SAS lads. I tried t' get him off, but couldn't. With half the Brit Army breathin up our arses, he begged me t' save myself, and I did. I heard later, before I left the country for Algiers, that one of ours was watchin' what happened from a roof across the street. He claims that a man we think is Brit MI5 executed your brother. Right there on the spot."

Megan felt herself shudder. She wrapped her arms tight to try and contain it. Her eyes closed, she felt tears squeeze out beneath the lids. When she opened them again, she saw Frankie had turned to watch her. "Y' just left him. Is that it?"

He stood his ground, his voice surprisingly gentle for a man of his reputation. "It's a war we're fightin', Megan. You know that. If I hadn't left, we'd both be dead right now. I did what I had t' do."

She nodded and turned away to gaze across the rink again. A shriek of laughter reached her. "They don't have any cares, do they? None of any consequence."

"Theirs is a different world," he replied. The knapsack that contained his cash was caught up with the toe of his shoe. One deft jerk of his knee and it leapt into his open hands. "Heavy, i'nt it?" he commented. "When did Fitzsimmons say the rest will be ready?"

She turned back to him with a rueful smile. "He didn't, but the crick in my neck from carryin' it is likely t' last me a week." After an instant's hesitation, she stuck her hand out to him again. "I s'pose I'd better be off then. Take care, Frankie."

This time, when Frankie caught hold of her hand, he held on to it. "Eight years, y' said it's been, Megan Desmond?"

She nodded.

"Y've become a right beautiful woman. With a lovely singin' voice, too."

Megan blushed, and Frankie McGuire leaned to kiss her on the cheek, still holding her hand.

"Ta, Megan Desmond." He gave her hand a tight squeeze before releasing it. Then he turned, hoisted the knapsack onto one shoulder, and disappeared into the night.

If Rory Devaney had wondered at all what it might feel like to carry two million dollars in cash aboard a New York City subway, and on the ferry from Manhattan to Staten Island, it wasn't something he dwelled on. Surely, he knew what it was he had wedged on the floor between his feet as he sat, but uppermost on his mind throughout that trip home was the woman he'd just met. By all the saints, he would swear she was the most beautiful creature he'd ever laid eyes upon. And Dessie Desmond's little sister, no less. Last night, before he ever saw her face, her voice had smitten him to the core of his romantic Irish soul. And with the face attached to that voice, he'd come as near to losing his heart as ever in his life. Tonight's meeting made the ache of emptiness he'd felt of late all the more difficult to bear. For the past month, he'd convinced himself all he needed was mere female companionship. Tonight, he'd discovered it wasn't the company of any female he craved. Just the company of one.

Too late for supper at the O'Mearas' once again, Rory had stopped for a burger and french fries in Times Square before the scheduled meet. Now, as he returned to his adopted family, he found the O'Meara women scurrying to and from the dining room and kitchen, cleaning up. As soon as little Annie saw him, she set the bowl she was carrying on the table and ran to leap into his arms.

"Rory! I can't make the ball bounce on my foot, no matter how hard I practice. My friend Livia says only boys can do it, and I'm stupid to even try."

With the knapsack of cash still on his back, Devaney hoisted the girl high to kiss her on the tip of her nose. He then set her on her feet again. "Rubbish. Tell your friend she's a ninny. Of course girls can do it."

She placed hands on her hips, scowled, and stamped one foot. "But I practice all the time."

"Then it'll come, love. Just you wait."

Bridget entered the dining room to grab the bowl her little sister had left behind. After the other night, when Rory failed to join her downstairs and groove to the Counting Crows, she'd behaved with cool remove around him.

"Hi, Bridge," he greeted her, and reached to the inside pocket of his coat. From it, he extracted the new U2 CD, purchased that afternoon at the Times Square Virgin Records superstore. "I thought Christmas might be too late for this, so I got it for y' now."

He might as well have handed her the Hope diamond. In her surprise, she nearly dropped the bowl. "You got that for me?"

His eyebrows went up. "Why not. Y' said y' were a big fan."

"And what did you get for me?" Annie demanded.

"All the world's love and affection, kiddo. Y've got to excuse me a moment while I run downstairs and wash up." He pointed to the CD now in Bridget's hands. "A little later, if your mother doesn't mind, we'll put that on the big stereo and turn it up a bit."

He left the older sister dumbfounded, and the younger one pouting, to hurry downstairs to his lair. As always, he took five minutes to check the area around his bed, and then the bathroom, for any sign of items having been disturbed. Old habits died hard. Then he stripped out of the sweater and shirt he'd worn since that morning's trip to Jones Beach, and ran water in the shower. Fifteen minutes later, with his hair combed, and dressed in jeans and a T-shirt, he settled down on the bathroom floor to secrete his cash in the hiding place he'd created.

Yesterday afternoon, with Tom gone off to work, Sheila away at her office, and the girls still in school, Rory had carefully chipped the grout from between two floor tiles beneath his dirty clothes hamper. Once he pried the tiles loose from the mastic that secured them, he'd used a battery-powered drill from the tugboat project, along with a keyhole saw, to cut a one-by-two-foot hole in the subfloor planking. The opening he'd created was barely big enough to accept that overstuffed knapsack. He had a moment's panic, trying to wedge it through.

"Rory?" It was Annie, on the stairs and headed his way.

With those loose tiles and pieces of subfloor still stacked alongside the opening to his cache, Devaney reached back with a foot to kick the bathroom door closed. "I'm in the bath, love!" he called out to her. "Out in a jiff!"

Not ten feet away, she replied, "I want you to see my dress. It's for Morgan's confirmation tomorrow."

Oh, Jesus. With everything else that had happened that past few days, it had completely slipped his mind. Morgan was being confirmed the next afternoon, a Saturday. The O'Mearas were throwing a grand party, with every relative and work associate invited from miles around. Right here, in this house. The subfloor replaced, he fit the two tiles back where they belonged and took just an instant to study them. With the hamper set back in its accustomed spot, a soul could sit there on the commode, stare right at it, and never be any the wiser.

12

◆

The morning of Morgan O'Meara's confirmation dawned as cold and crisp as it had the previous day. Unable to push his own project any further until Pete Fitzsimmons came up with the additional cash to meet Billy Burke's full price, Rory Devaney allowed himself to sleep an extra hour. Sean had wanted him to come into the city to carouse the bars and late-night clubs, but he'd begged off. The prospect of an open ocean voyage in a sixty-foot boat with a crew of two had him a bit on edge. The fact that Fitzsimmons was unable to come up with the entire three million also gave him pause. He wanted to get on with this. Soon. Before he did something reckless like asking Megan Desmond to go with him.

In an attempt to get his mind off Megan, the

money, and his trip, Rory joined Sheila O'Meara for a brisk three-mile walk. All of the leaves were off the huge maples lining most of the neighborhood streets now, and everywhere they went residents were at work getting leaves into piles and bags. They stopped for fresh bagels on the last leg home, and arrived back to find the house in a state of anxious preparation. A neighborhood deli had prepared several huge platters of cold cuts, pans of lasagna and ziti, and cheese boards fit to feed a horde. Tom had laid them out on the two long tables he'd rented for the occasion. Meanwhile, all the girls were upstairs, dressing for church. Morgan and Bridget were fighting over the bath.

"Y' need a hand, Tom, just point where," Rory offered as he hung his jacket.

"Toast me one of those bagels," O'Meara replied. "I can smell them from here. Big smear of cream cheese."

"Done."

"Mom!" Bridget hollered down the stairs. "Morgan's been in the Gee Dee bathroom for over half an hour. She stays in there much longer, I'm going to look like shit!"

"Watch your mouth, young lady!" Tom hollered back. "It's her confirmation. Leave her alone."

"Why?" Bridget complained. "She could spend another hour in there, and it won't make her look any better."

"I heard that!" Morgan screamed from behind the closed bathroom door.

Rory chuckled and started for the kitchen with the bag of bagels. "One for you, too, Sheila?" he asked.

"No cream cheese," she replied. "I'll never get into my dress."

In the kitchen, Devaney found little Annie already decked out in her white-and-blue pinafore, her hair done in pigtails with ribbons the blue of her dress. "Y' look very pretty, young lady," he complimented, bowing from the waist. "Who did your hair?"

She looked up from the bowl of cereal she was eating. "My daddy did. He can braid."

"So I see. Very impressive t' have a father so useful as that."

She nodded, her expression deadly serious. "And a mommy like mine, too. Why aren't you married, Rory?"

He placed the bag of bagels on the counter, extracted three and found a bread knife to slice them. " 'Tis not as easy t' find the right girl as y' think."

Spoon gripped in one fist the way a child so often holds one, she frowned. "What about me? I'd marry you. I'm going to be even prettier than my sister Bridget when I grow up."

He popped two bagel halves into the toaster as he laughed. "Indeed, I bet perhaps y' will."

She dropped her spoon to the table and jammed those tiny fists to her hips. "Why are you laughing?" she demanded. "It's true."

"Because y' delight me so, young one."

"So will you marry me?"

In that moment, Rory realized how much he'd come to love this child, and her whole family. Tom O'Meara, a policeman of all things, his vivacious wife, and their wonderfully lively and complex brood. "I'd be honored, sweet lass," he replied. "If y' think you've got patience t' wait for a footloose scoundrel like me."

Though baptized a Catholic, and certainly persecuted for being one, in a land where the line that divided was clear and simple, Rory Devaney hadn't been to a mass in over ten years. Not even to a funeral mass. In Belfast, his exploits were well enough known by the time he was seventeen to prevent him from ever showing his face at a public gathering. And if the truth be known, the day he'd seen his da shot dead, he'd forever lost his faith in a wise and merciful God. In a place where many of his neighbors hated him, not for who he was, but what he was, how could he love them as himself? In the face of maltreatment and ruthless aggression, how could he meekly turn the other cheek? In Ireland, the meek had inherited nothing. Not contentment, not justice, and certainly not the earth.

In this country where religious tolerance was one of the foundation stones of the republic, the experience of sitting in a church was so alien to Rory that he felt as though he were drifting through a dream. Not as ancient as so many of the structures in his native land, the O'Mearas' parish church was built of a granitelike stone, with a high, vaulted ceiling, stained-glass windows depicting the stations of the cross, and two little side chapels in the wings, with their own separate altars and banks of flickering votive candles. There was a huge gothic sanctuary behind the main communion rail, and because this was a confirmation, performed by a bishop in full regalia, the mass was a high mass. There were two other priests and a legion of acolytes in attendance. The air was full of the smoke of burning incense, evoking strong memories of that funeral for his father, so long ago. The flashbacks it triggered in Rory's mind were vividly primal. The IRA soldier was far removed from his conflict, and at peace for a moment. He was moved so strongly by this setting and its sensory assault that he nearly wept.

When everyone around him started to rise and file toward the communion rail, Rory was so lost in his own thoughts that he failed, at first, to realize what was happening. Then he saw Sheila looking at him, her expression a mixture of confusion and concern.

"You feeling okay?" she whispered as she stood. "You look a little peaked."

"I'm fine, ta," he dismissed her concern. And shifting in the pew, he moved his knees from her path.

"You're not receiving communion?"

He met her eyes, smiled slightly, and shook his head no.

"Watch Annie?"

He reached down to take the child's hand. "Of course."

As Annie's mother and father shuffled past and out into the aisle to join the stream of communicants, the child leaned close to Rory. "Why didn't you go?"

"Sometimes you don't go if you don't feel right," he replied.

"You're sick?" She asked it loud enough that several people in nearby pews turned their heads.

"No, no. I'm fine," he whispered.

Annie scowled. "But you just said you don't feel good."

He squeezed her hand and smiled. "I said I don't feel right. There's a difference."

At home, even with all the troubles, any event like a christening, first communion, confirmation, wedding, or wake called for a gathering of family and friends. Rory Devaney was surprised by how familiar the party at Tom and Sheila O'Meara's house felt to him. Though the setting, food, and faces were different, large Irish families were apparently boisterous and noisy the world round. Here like there, they had a fondness for drink, food, and laughter. Within fifteen minutes of his return to the house from church, Rory's head was filled with the names of so many aunts, uncles, cousins, and friends that he gave up all hope of remembering them. Surprised, at first, to learn that Tom's partner was Hispanic, and that several of the men invited from his command were black, Rory took a moment to wonder why he should be. He admired the ease with which O'Meara welcomed each of them and their wives into his home, and the grace with which Sheila circulated among them, making introductions.

"Rory?" It was Bridget, at his elbow, standing awkwardly with a tall, well-built redheaded boy. "I would, uh, like you to meet Kevin."

For the past week or so, Morgan had been overheard making snide remarks about some new boyfriend. They'd been tinged with more than a little obvious jealousy, and now Rory could see why. The boy would never be a matinee idol, but was a handsome, strapping specimen with a naturally bemused twist to his mouth, and mischief in his eyes.

"Pleased to meet you, sir," the kid greeted him. The grip of his handshake was impressive.

Devaney frowned and looked back over his shoulder. "Sir, is it? I thought my grand da might be standing behind me."

When he laughed, the self-conscious boy brayed a bit like a donkey. At his side, Bridget colored. She and her attempt at sophisticated cool were already on thin ice.

"You both go t' the same school?" Rory asked.

That got him another of those laughs. "St. John Villa's all girls," Kevin informed him. "I'm a freshman at St. John's University. In Queens."

"Ah. A college man."

Kevin stood a little taller. "Yes, sir."

Rory reached to take one of the kid's elbows with an easy hand and leaned close to whisper in his ear.

"Y' don't lay off the sir shit, I'm gonna strangle y'."

Eyes gone wide, the younger man stepped back a pace to stare at this curiosity, trying to determine whether or not he was serious. Rory winked at him and suggested they head over to the beverage table.

Rory spotted Tom O'Meara in conversation with his partner, Eddie Diaz, as he stopped to pluck a bottled extra stout from a washtub full of ice, beer, and soda. The partner's girlfriend looked bored, standing a bit to one side. Rory considered stepping over to chat her up when Tom broke away to approach him. It wasn't until O'Meara arrived that Devaney realized that boyfriend Kevin was the object of his host's attention, and not him. Without missing a beat, Tom grabbed a can of Coca-Cola from the ice, handed it to the boy, took the Budweiser from his hand, and said thanks. Rory had to give the surprised kid credit. He was quick-witted.

"My pleasure, sir. Nice party."

"That's Sergeant to you, junior," O'Meara growled. "As in sworn to uphold the law. Like the one against underage drinking."

Judging from Tom's expression, Rory was surprised he didn't also mention statutory rape. But then again, Rory wasn't a father, forced to watch a hormone-charged young stud drool over the fruit of his loins. It was a phenomenon that could no doubt sour a man's good humor.

Eddie Diaz had also watched the exchange between his boss and Bridget's new boyfriend. When

O'Meara returned to his side, beer in hand. he shook his head and chuckled.

"I know you don't wanna hear this, Sarge, but that kinda shit ain't never gonna help your cause, It's exactly opposite of everything thirty years on the street has taught you."

"Fuck you talking about?" O'Meara demanded.

"Not the bullshit with the beer, but how you pulled the bully stunt in front of Bridget like that. She wanted to crawl in a hole."

"Maybe she'd be safer in a hole."

Eddie grunted. "She's a good-looking woman, Sarge. Look at her. It ain't just him. It's every guy who'll ever get a shot at her. You can't stand the idea of it."

"Jesus H," O'Meara complained. "That's my daughter you're talking about, Diaz."

"Nuh-uh," Eddie countered. He shook his head. "It's you I'm talking about, Tom. You push her like that, she'll turn right around an' do the opposite of what you tell her, out of spite."

Tom tried to defend himself. "So what am I supposed to do? Stand aside and condone that kind of behavior in my own fucking house?"

"What behavior? He was gonna have a beer. What? You never had a beer, your whole freshman year in college?"

"That's not the point," Tom snapped.

Eddie smiled. "Which is exactly mine. And by the way, I think it's about time you give up this other bullshit, too. Gimme the keys Monday, and let me drive."

O'Meara had started to walk off. He stopped and turned. "Is that all you've been angling at?" His tone was heavy with disbelief.

Eddie met it head-on. "You think that, you didn't listen to one word I just said."

It was such a nice autumn day, with the weather at least ten degrees warmer than it had been all week, that Rory decided to absent himself from the party awhile and sit in the sunshine on the porch. He wanted to savor everything about his setting; the quiet, peaceful street; the fun-loving chatter and laughter emanating from the house at his back; the feeling of being fueled by something other than hatred. All of these things he wanted to capture and tuck away in some private place. He wanted to remember the tangy smell of these fallen leaves as vividly as the smell of that incense this morning at mass. This was the happiest he'd been since that day twenty years ago, when his da had let him take the helm of their boat. Twenty years. The gulf was so deep and wide between here and there that he wondered how he'd ever made the leap, and managed to survive.

Behind Devaney, the front door opened and closed again. He looked back to see Bridget's Kevin approach to stand on the stoop behind him.

"Mind if I join you?" the kid asked.

"Not a'tall. Seat yourself."

Kevin folded those lanky legs to sit and wrap his arms around his knees. "I get the distinct impression her old man doesn't like me," he said.

"She's his little girl," Rory replied. "You're the rogue kid come sniffin' round. The one who can break her heart, get her pregnant, ruin her life. I doubt it's easy bein' any girl's father, let alone a pretty one's." He handed Kevin his beer.

The younger lad took the offered bottle without appearing to think about it. When he had a long pull and continued to hang on to it, Devaney reached across to gently take it back.

"Y' like her?" Rory asked softly.

Kevin nodded. "Met her last year at a football game. Thought she was cute, but kinda stuck-up. Then I met her again at a party last week. It was mostly college kids. She and her friend hardly knew anyone. We just started talking."

"And sort of hit it off, right?"

Kevin's expression became animated. "She likes the same music I do. Loves the Anne Rice vampire books, and Stephen King. We can talk for hours."

It sounded to Rory like as good a basis for a relationship as any, and better than most. "Judging from how you were droolin' in there, I expect y' think she's pretty, too."

"God," Kevin groaned. "Was I that obvious?"

"You're what? Nineteen? Of course you were obvious. And that's the sort of thing make's her da's hair stand on end."

The door behind them opened again, and this time Annie poked her head out. "Rory. It's the telephone. Another man who talks funny, just like you."

Inside the house, they'd rolled back the living room carpet for dancing. Morgan, another of her schoolmates, and an older man played jig music on two fiddles and a flute. Sheila O'Meara was arm-in-arm in the middle of the room with her parish priest, having a grand time. She spotted Rory and signaled for him to come join the fun. He made a talking-on-the-phone gesture and followed Annie into the kitchen.

"What's all the noise?" Sean asked when he picked up.

"Morgan's confirmation party. Speak up, I can barely hear y'."

"Get to a secure line and call me back," Sean replied. "I'm at my place. Something's come up."

The public phone nearest to the O'Meara house was at the end of the block and around the corner at a laundry. Rory told Sean he'd get back to him shortly, hurried downstairs to find quarters, and upstairs again to slip out the back door. Breathless after his sprint down the back alley to the end of the block, he had plenty of time to recover as a woman with a baby in a stroller monopolized the laundry phone for close to ten minutes.

"What took y'?" Sean demanded when Rory finally reached him. He sounded tense. It was not his usual demeanor.

"Never mind. Tell me what's happened."

"The Brits've killed Martin McDuff. Flushed him out of the deepest hole he had. A cabin on Sketrick Island, in Strangford Lough. Shot him down like a fookin' dog."

Devaney knew Strangford Lough well. A large inland bay, the north end of which was situated ten miles east of Belfast, it encompassed a shoreline dotted with dozens of tiny islands. The IRA had used it as a refuge for years. "How does that affect our plans here?" he asked.

"Fitzsimmons is freaking, Frankie. I got a call not more'n an hour ago from McDuff's contact, Megan Desmond. She sounds scared, too. Wants t' meet wit y' and talk. Tomorrow mornin' at a museum at the north tip o' Manhattan called the Cloisters."

While studying the part of the city were Tom O'Meara worked his beat, Rory had seen the Cloisters on his map. "What time?"

"She said eleven. T' meet her in the herb garden."

Besides being beautiful, Megan Desmond was Devaney's only conduit to the additional million dollars they needed to meet Billy Burke's price. "Fine," he said. "And remember, Sean. If McDuff was compromised, we may be, as well. Watch your arse."

13

◆

Pieces of several medieval monasteries purchased by the Rockefeller family, then reassembled in Ft. Tryon Park on behalf of the Metropolitan Museum of Art, the Cloisters sat high on a bluff overlooking the Hudson River. That Sunday morning, temperatures had plummeted again, and the sky above was one heavy mass of damp gray. Open since nine-thirty A.M., the museum had already attracted a surprising number of visitors for such a dreary day, but then everywhere Rory traveled in New York City, the volume of traffic, both pedestrian and auto, continued to astonish him.

Rory found Megan in the herb garden. Most of the garden was put to bed for the winter. She loitered casually at one corner of a path, eavesdropping on a tour guide. As he approached her, Rory felt his heart skip in the same disconcerting way it had on that staircase three nights ago, and then again Friday night in Central Park. When she looked up to meet his eyes, he saw fear.

"I was worried y' might not come," she said.

He took her hand, and together they started down the path toward a more remote area of the garden.

"Y' really think they might be close?" he asked. He found it hard to imagine. Martin McDuff was nothing if he wasn't cautious. So far as Rory knew, he kept no files, no records of who any of his contacts were, or where.

"The jooge thinks they might be. He's scared witless. He says that if they could smoke Martin out, we've sprung a hole in our security bigger than the one that sank the *Titanic*."

"Frightened how?" Rory pressed her. "What has he done?"

"Packed Juliet and little Molly off to their house near Woodstock in the Catskills."

Rory felt a strange, stranded sort of panic start to build in him. If this was all it took to scare Pete Fitzsimmons, he was happy to know it now. "What about the rest of our money, Megan?"

"I don't know, Frankie. The way I've seen Jooge Pete actin', I don't think y' can count on it anymore."

Rory's mouth drew tight. He stared off over the Hudson to the sheer cliffs of the Palisades on the New Jersey side.

"Is that it, then?" Megan asked. "Is it finished?"

Frankie thought of all the work they'd done on the boat, and then thought of the two million dollars in stateside donations sitting in the damp beneath Tom O'Meara's basement bathroom. As his anger rose, he had to force himself to sit on it, drive it back down. He was a soldier on a mission. In war, the cool head more often won the day. "By no means," he murmured.

"So what'll y' do with only two thirds o' the money?"

He pursed his lips and shrugged. "Make Billy Burke see reason, I s'pose. But it's to no good end if we've no longer got McDuff's support on the Portrush end." He paused, thinking fast and hard. "Somehow, I've got t' fly t' Europe and sneak back into Belfast. I'm convinced it was no one in my Falls Road bunch who got your brother and those others killed. It's some other unit that's sprung the leak. I'll gather my own handpicked lot."

"Y' can't show your face in Belfast now, Frankie," she argued. "Y' do, you're a dead man."

"I wasn't planning t' show my face, Megan love."

She held her breath a long moment. As she studied him, she was clearly trying to make up her mind about something. "Let me go instead," she blurted. "Tell me who t' see. What t' say. I'm Dessie's sister. They'll trust me. And y' know you can trust me, too."

Devaney was apprehensive. In this war they waged, he'd known many a valiant female soldier.

Some of whom had sacrificed their lives for the cause. But Megan was unblooded. "You'd be willin' t' get that involved?"

"I'm already involved," she insisted. "I've been Martin's contact with our people here for these past three years. They've killed my brother, Frankie."

He studied her in this new light, impressed with the earnestness he saw. Then he smiled and reached to caress her cheek with the side of this thumb. "All right then, Megan Desmond. It's you we'll send t' Belfast. Me we'll send back t' Billy Burke."

Devaney stood in the cold outside the window to Burke's Bar for close to fifteen minutes. Its proprietor was not only present that Sunday afternoon, but very much enjoying himself, and Rory took that time outside on the sidewalk to study the man, what sort of public image he liked to project when he wasn't conducting his other business. Today, Burke had his sights set on an attractive brunette of thirty-five or so. Long legs in a very short skirt; cashmere sweater not tight enough to be in poor taste; a pretty, pug-nosed Irish face. Burke worked his charms while standing beside her bar stool, his whisky within easy reach, as well as one of her long slender thighs. Even as other patrons made demands on his attentions, he spent as much time stroking that thigh as he did his drink, his body language proclaiming that he was with her. The crowd seemed docile and thirsty enough to make him happy. The woman seemed eager enough to accept his advances, which made him happy, too. Teddy, so far as Rory could determine, was nowhere in evidence.

It was interesting to watch Billy's face tighten for just an instant when he first spotted Rory entering his establishment. The tightness was replaced, a heartbeat later, with his jovial, proprietor's smile as he leaned over to whisper something in the brunette's ear. Without looking Devaney's way, she nodded, kissed Burke on the cheek, and hopped from her stool to head toward the ladies' room. With a glance at Rory, he picked up his drink and started back through the dining room toward his office. Halfway up the stairs, he looked back over his shoulder.

"I just heard about Martin this morning."

Rory wondered how surprised he should be. As deep under as he was, there was no way to know how widely the news had circulated.

Burke led the way into his office and indicated the leather sofa. He took his desk chair. "Was there family?" he asked.

"Aye. A wife and two little ones."

"Given the circumstances, I'm sure you're here to say you need to postpone. That would pose quite an inconvenience."

"Just long enough t' get matters at home straightened out," Rory countered. "No more n' two weeks, at most."

Burke seemed dubious. "You could work it that fast? With a security leak of this magnitude? How can you be sure you've plugged it?"

Devaney shrugged. "I guess that's our problem, not yours, Mr. Burke. From you, we need missiles."

"Fine. Make payment, I'll store them for you."

"We've got a little problem there, too," Rory allowed. "We're still a bit short."

Burke scowled now. "These ain't soda cans you asked me to find you. Jesus. How short? I'm out some serious dollars here."

"One third."

"A million bucks?" Burke feigned a stricken look. "Holy Christ! These things are worth three million at fucking bargain-basement rates. You got any idea how much I'm out here?"

Devaney refused to rise to Burke's bait. The man was a self-confessed amateur actor, after all. He kept his tone direct and cool. "I'm sure it's nowhere near the three million we promised y', Billy."

It was the first time in their relationship that he'd called Burke by his first name. The weapons merchant didn't fail to catch it. "You're fuckin' with me," he growled.

Rory shook his head. "Negative. All our cash conduits've shut down. Imagine the reactions t' this news in Boston, the North Bronx, and every other Irish stronghold on this side of the big spit. Martin McDuff was a ghost. Unreachable."

"Well they reached him, didn't they," Burke said.

"We'll get y' the rest of the money," Rory assured him. "It'll just take a bit more time. Or, if y' really do want that statue of St. Burke erected in Donegall Place? Y' could agree t' take the two million we've already got in hand."

Burke's eyes bulged. "My bleeding butt I could. The price is the same, wiseass."

"Fine." Rory rose to leave. "I do love the heart of a mercenary, Billy. Y' always know just how fervently it beats. Don't offer me a drink on my way out. I'd be tempted t' throw it in your face."

Monday morning saw Sean Geary arrive at the Arthur Kill boatyard in the company of Megan Desmond. Through the tugboat's wheelhouse windscreen, Rory watched the two of them make their way toward him down the dock. It was still cold and miserable out, with the sky threatening rain and sleet. Devaney had fired up the boat's generator to take the damp chill out of the cabin interior. He'd also put a kettle to boil on the galley stove. Soon they would have tea.

Their plan that day was a simple one. While Rory and Megan went over the plans and organizational charts he'd worked late into the night preparing, Sean would return to Manhattan to watch Burke's place for any sign of suspicious activity. If the weapons dealer went anywhere, Geary was to follow at a discreet distance. He had orders to procure a Polaroid camera and take photographs of anyone Burke met, and any establishments he might visit. Like Rory, Sean was an old hand at clandestine surveillance. In Belfast, before any attack was launched on British Army or Ulster Volunteer Force positions, members of the Provisional IRA spent weeks doing background checks on individual targets, and exhaustive area surveys.

"Looks t' me like rank's got its definite fookin' privileges," Geary grumbled as he delivered Megan into the warmth of the tugboat's interior. "I shag arse across the cold, windy streets of Gotham, while you and this lovely bird nest up here like a couple of turtledoves."

"Is he always so charming as this?" Megan asked Devaney. "The entire trip out here, he did nothing but grouse. About the weather. About how the women of this city fail t' understand him. That, and the sufferin' baby jaysus knows what else."

"He's jealous that you get t' fly t' Belfast, and he's got t' sail there in this tub," Rory told her. "Man's got no sense of adventure." He didn't mention that Sean had also gone a bit green around the gills during their proving run on Raritan Bay last week. The prospect of a fifteen-day voyage across the open ocean was not sitting well with Geary at the moment. An excellent marine mechanic aboard boats tied up in port or in dry dock, Sean was no seaman.

"Adventure, my arse," Sean sneered. "You two enjoy your day t'gether. I'm sure you'll both miss me terribly."

Once Geary had departed, Rory wasted no time getting down to business. In the company of Megan Desmond, he thought it wisest to stay focused on the task at hand. They were at war, he continually reminded himself. Megan Desmond was a comrade in arms. His deeper feelings for her were of no use to the cause. Once revealed, they could only complicate an already dicey situation.

By late afternoon, as the sun began to set, Rory rose to stretch and brew up yet another pot of tea. Megan knew the name of every trusted Falls Road lad and those of their immediate families by heart now. She knew in precise detail the point of Devaney's proposed landfall east of Portrush, and the route the missiles would take south, first to Ballymoney, then Ballymena, Antrim, and on into the Belfast suburb of Hollywood, adjacent to the city's Harbour Airport.

With fresh tea bags dropped into the empty pot and the bottle-gas burner flame turned high, Rory switched on the small galley radio in hopes of getting the latest weather forecast. Before dusk, the sky had turned a nasty green-gray, suggesting the possibility of snow. At thirty-four degrees, the mercury steadily falling, conditions outside their snug little cabin were ideal for it.

"Give it to me again," he said. "From the beginning."

She stared at him. "You're joking. If we've been over it one time, we've been over it fif—"

"Again," he insisted.

In the singsong voice of an automaton, she began to once more rattle off her itinerary. "I fly New York t' Dublin. From Dublin I catch a bus t' Greenore. I cross the border by boat over Carlingford Lough t' Rostrevor. A fisherman named Sweeney, who I find in the little boat basin adjacent t' the Greenore lighthouse, will transport me. In Rostrevor, I catch a bus t' Belfast by way of Newry and Dromore. In Belfast,

I contact Billy Boyle through his sister Kathy, at her boat shop on Dufferin Road. Once I meet with Billy, I deliver your detailed plan, as fol—"

"All right, fine," Rory relented. "You've got it. I'm sure y' do."

"God, I hope so," she moaned, and threw her head back to roll the kinks out of her neck. "You're a hard taskmaster, Frankie McGuire."

"And I count myself among the living, thanks to it," he replied. "When this is all over, I want t' count you among the living, too, Megan Desmond."

She stared at him with a solemnity he hadn't yet seen in her that day. "It's not just a message I'm deliverin', but a death sentence t' dozens of Brit flyboys. I know it was their side killed my brother. Him and countless others. But do y' ever have second thoughts about all the killin', Frankie?"

The kettle began to boil. Rory took it off the flame to pour water over the tea bags. "It was Voltaire who said it, I believe. That killing a man is murder, unless it is done to the sound of trumpets. Well, I never heard a single note blown, the day those UVF bastards came t' my house, and shot down my da in cold blood." He paused to look deep into her eyes. "Second thoughts, Megan? Surely. In war, there are no innocents. Everyone has his ghosts."

The station he'd tuned to on the radio played a variety of so-called *alternative* rock and roll artists. When the first chords of Elvis Costello's "Tramp the Dirt Down" bit through the heaviness left by their last exchange, Megan brightened. "Turn that up, will y', Frankie?"

Devaney eased the volume higher and watched Megan close her eyes to sway with the beat. "Dance?" he murmured.

Her dimples deepened. Then her eyes came back open again, alive with intrigue and mischief. "Aye." She offered him her hand and he took it. She rose.

Their bodies made contact. "Y' smell wonderful," he murmured, his nose buried in her hair.

"Umm," she replied, and wrapped her arms around his neck to sway with him. "Y' feel good, Frankie."

"And you, t' me, Megan Desmond."

The cabin was lit by a sudden, silent flash of brilliant white light. Both dancers were so caught off guard that neither could react. Their breathing, and for an instant perhaps, their hearts, stopped as one. And then, in the next moment, Rory was a blur of instinctive response. A foot swept at Megan's ankles to knock her off balance. He drove her with him to the deck, his body thrown across hers to shield her as he clawed for the weapon jammed into his waistband beneath his sweater.

"Gotcha!" Sean Geary bellowed, then roared with laughter at the effectiveness of his prank.

Rory had the pistol cleared and half brought around to bear before he realized who the interloper was. He stopped, and when he looked up from where he and Megan lay, he saw Geary at the wheelhouse door. Sean had a Polaroid camera in one hand, and a six-pack of beer wedged beneath his other arm. As Geary advanced into the cabin, he set the beer on the galley table and plucked the photograph from the front of his camera.

"You bloody fookin' bastard!" Rory seethed.

Sean laughed again and handed the developing snapshot to him. "Keep it t' show your kiddies, it ever comes t' that. I'm sure it's a cracker, unless there's too much glare from the flash off the glass."

14

Tom O'Meara and Eddie Diaz were back working days that week. It was after lunch, Tuesday, and Diaz was so content after his meal of chicken fried steak and gravied mash potatoes, he'd failed to make his usual fuss about driving. The sarge had the wheel, and both of them scanned the streets as they rolled. It had become a habit for both men by now, the always watching, ever on the alert for the slightest thing out of whack in their world. They turned the corner from Broadway onto Dyckman Street.

"Three years from today, I'll have my twenty in," Diaz announced. He shook his head in amazement. "Some days it seems like I've been at this job forever. Others, I can't imagine how the time has flown

169

by so fast." He glanced in O'Meara's direction. "Know what I mean?"

His gaze still on the street before them, Tom smiled. It *was* hard to believe that Eddie Diaz had seventeen years in, today. It seemed like yesterday he'd first met him as a young rookie patrolman, working out of the 203rd station house in Jamaica, Queens. When they'd reconnected here, three years ago, it seemed impossible that fourteen years had passed. Today, Diaz still had hardly a line in his face, while O'Meara felt like one of the job's dinosaurs.

"How old are you now, Eddie?"

"Thirty-eight, next March."

"You're soundin' like you get your twenty, you plan to put in your papers. True?"

Diaz stared out the passenger-side window at the desperate grime of the surrounding tenements. This was Dominican land up here, with a few die-hard immigrant Jews still holding on. It was too cold now for the card tables outside bodegas, old men passing their days playing dominoes. These Caribbean folk hated the cold, and mostly stayed indoors from here to April unless they were forced out onto the streets by necessity. Out of groceries, or off to midtown and some sweatshop job. How hard could it be to leave all this behind, Eddie wondered? With a guaranteed thirty-four thousand dollars a year, New York State tax free.

"Just might," he allowed. "I been thinking 'bout potbellied pigs."

"Say what?"

"Potbellied pigs. I saw this show on the Discovery Channel about a month back. About how some sonofabitch is making a fortune breeding these little fucking pigs . . . right over the river in Jersey somewhere."

"Pigs."

"Little pigs. For pets, man. Had them in this kennel-type setup. Sells 'em to parents to give to their kids on birthdays and shit. Cute as hell."

"You're talking about pigs, Eddie. What kinda second career is that. What? You been going to vet school nights and not told me about it?"

A couple of teenage girls on the street waved at Eddie and he waved back, then shifted in his seat to face O'Meara. He was excited about the concept now. "Vietnamese pigs. Potbellies. You ain't heard about them? They're s'pose to be smart as hell, and real clean, too. This guy was getting five hundred a pop for them."

"I see. I didn't realize you were talking about clean pigs. That makes all the difference in the world." Tom couldn't contain the smile that crept out from the corners of his mouth. "What happened to the bakery, Eddie? I thought you wanted to bake bread, and cakes, and pies and all. This sounds even more harebrained than that." Tom gestured toward Diaz's side of the car. "Watch the goddamn street."

Eddie shifted back around, his expression one of frustration. Sure he'd floated a few lame retirement career ideas, but how many pets could you raise that you could eat if you got tired of them? This thing had potential. Big time. "You got any idea what time a man's gotta haul his ass outta bed to bake bread?" he grumbled.

Tom chuckled. "Everything's got a downside."

As soon as Diaz got himself situated facing forward again, something odd caught his eye on the sidewalk up the block. A young Hispanic male in a black watch cap and Oakland Raiders satin jacket had something he was adjusting furtively in the fingers of one gloved hand. In the next instant, he glanced quickly back and forth, failed to see the approaching patrol car, and swung the object at the passenger-side window of a parked five-series BMW.

"Spark plugger," Diaz grunted, and reached for the door release.

It was the latest cute trick employed by urban street kids to steal CDs, CD players, and other valuables found lying around inside parked cars. The tip of a spark plug was high-carbon steel. When focused correctly, it could shatter safety glass even more effectively than a metal bar or rock. An added bonus was the spark plug's size. It was easy to conceal, and just as easy to throw away.

"Wait for me to get around him," O'Meara told him. "Take the radio." But Eddie was already out of the moving car and running at a crouch past the row of parked cars to where that kid now leaned inside the violated Beemer.

Without thinking about it Tom had the radio in

his hand. "Central, this is unit twelve-oh-seven. We've got a ten twenty-two GLA in progress on Dyckman. Two blocks east of Broadway. Give me a ten eighty-five, one unit on the back. Over."

"That's a ten-four, twelve-oh-seven," the dispatcher responded. "Ten twenty-two Grand Larceny Attempt. Backup is en route. Over."

O'Meara continued to ease the car up the block as Eddie sneaked closer to the perp. Apparently, the thief was having trouble getting at what he wanted. Right there in broad daylight, he'd crawled halfway in through the window of the car. His head was seen bobbing frantically up and down as he jerked at something. Doper, Tom thought. Probably a pipe-head.

Oscar Delacruz was having another bad day. Winter was coming, Oscar was two weeks behind on his rent, he was out of rock for his pipe, and some bitch named Linda, or Belinda, or something was claiming he was the father of the baby she carried. Oscar needed quick cash, first to get his head straight, and second to buy a ticket back to the D.R. He wanted out of this nightmare, New York. Anyone who said the living would be easy here, with cars, easy women, and nights of dancing, was full of shit. For three years he'd worked at least ten different jobs pushing carts around garment district streets, never getting one inch ahead. The car he'd bought was a fifteen-year-old Ford Fairmont, now dead and abandoned on some side street. The women were the same as they were back home: ballbusters, every last one. And the only music he could afford to hear most nights came from a six-dollar clock radio in his one-room tenement hovel. Six months ago, Oscar had said to hell with it, and gone on the pipe. It was the best decision he'd made since coming here. If he couldn't prosper, at least he could take vacations in his head.

The spark-plug trick was something another guy from the D.R. had taught him a couple months back. Spot some juicy item left lying in plain sight on a car seat, then one quick little tap with the tip of a plug and it was yours. Oscar had started out just grabbing Discmans, shopping bags, and loose CDs. Then, about a month ago, the dude he sold those portable CD players to, said he could do much better if he moved up a notch to the installed sound systems. Just cut the mounting bracket with tin snips, and rip the whole thing out, loose wiring and all.

The white BMW had a nice unit. Pioneer, with a three-disc magazine. Oscar had just been wandering idly when he glanced in the car window. Once he spotted the sweet rig in there, he couldn't help himself. He never went anywhere without a plug and pair of snips anymore.

Once he'd gained entrance to the car, Oscar quickly discovered that this particular mounting bracket was a type he'd never encountered before. He tried to cut it with the snips, but the damned thing just laughed at them. Hard as a rock dealer's

heart, it gave him nothing but frustration as he
jerked and tore at it. Finally, giving up, he looked
desperately around for something, *anything*, to
steal.

The glove box was where Delacruz found the zip-
pered leather pouch. Bingo. It had a little Semmerling 9 mm automatic inside, a sweet little hideaway
piece worth twice to him what that radio would
bring. Maybe as much as a hundred dollars. With
the leather pouch abandoned and the gun in one
hand, Oscar backed out of the window, shattered
glass crunching underfoot.

Tom O'Meara had stopped, two cars back of the
BMW, while Eddie Diaz snuck up on that idiot
crackhead, so busy with his business he was oblivious to the rest of the world. Lucky for the thief, the
car's owner didn't appear. Anybody who drove a
528 BMW in this neighborhood was likely to kill
the man found breaking into his precious wheels.
Cops would only arrest him.

As Diaz started around the rear of the car to get a
drop on the guy, Tom eased the cruiser forward to
seal off any avenue escape. That was when O'Meara
saw the gun in the perp's right hand.

"Down, Eddie! Gun!" he yelled out the open passenger-side window. When he threw his door open
and started to leap from the car, a passing motorist
had to swerve with a scream of rubber on pavement
to avoid hitting him.

On the sidewalk, the perp heard the warning shout

and then saw Eddie's head as Diaz dove for cover. In a panic, the thief aimed wildly and loosed two shots in Eddie's direction. Then he turned, to flee east down the block.

Tom felt that telltale twinge in his knee again as he ran, crouched low, to Eddie's side.

"You okay?" he shouted.

"Fine. Let's get that fucker."

In the next moment both cops were up and running in hot pursuit. At the corner of Nagle Avenue, the perp took the turn too hard as he tried to double back toward Broadway, and fell. He was up again in an instant, but limping slightly as he threw a quick glance back over his shoulder. Eddie's fondness for fried food notwithstanding, he was gaining on the guy. The older O'Meara was just a pace or two off his lead. Halfway up the short block between Dyckman Street and Thayer, O'Meara saw the perp toss something into an open doorway. Eddie continued to give chase while he dodged into the entry to grab what it was. The gun.

O'Meara turned quickly to resume his pursuit as two loud reports rang out. On the sidewalk, the other side of Thayer Street, he saw Diaz standing stunned, his service weapon in his right hand. He stared down at the fallen suspect, still convulsing in the throes of death. There wasn't any question in Tom's mind that his partner had shot and killed the man, more than likely unarmed. Suddenly he was sick to his stomach.

* * *

As Eddie Diaz watched the young Latino die at his feet, a strange numbness slowly crept over him. "This ain't happening," a voice in his head insisted. "Not to me. Where's the fucking gun?"

Everywhere Eddie looked on the sidewalk around the dying man, the weapon which had fired those two shots at him back on Dyckman was no longer in evidence. In desperation, he dropped to one knee and shoved the quivering corpse onto its back, hoping the dumb shit had fallen on it. But no. The gun wasn't there, either.

"What happened?" the sarge gasped as he rushed up.

I dunno," Eddied replied hollowly. "All of a sudden he stopped and started t' turn. I thought . . ." He let it trail off.

"Jesus, Eddie," Tom complained. "You shot him in the fucking back. You didn't see him toss the gun?"

Diaz looked up at him blankly. "Bullshit, boss. He was turning. He was gonna . . ." And then he saw the weapon in O'Meara's hand. "Oh Jesus. Where?"

The sarge jerked a thumb over his shoulder. "Doorway back there."

Eddie felt the blood drain from his face. If this was a back alley, somewhere out of plain sight, a cop in a jam like this could flip a corpse over and shoot it again in front, claim the first shot had spun him, and the second two caught him in the back. But here, onlookers were already starting to gather in doorways up and down Nagle Avenue. More stared down at them from windows in surrounding buildings. There was a good chance that someone had seen Tom retrieve the discarded weapon from that doorway. On the other hand, Eddie could see no other choice. He had to take the only chance he had.

O'Meara looked at him, incredulous, when he reached to pluck that little five-shot Semmerling automatic from Tom's hand.

"What are you doin', Eddie?"

"Returning property to its rightful owner. Paraffin tests'll prove he took those two shots at me. So will this." He shielded the corpse with his body, and wedged the gun with his knee beneath the dead man's right hip.

The sarge didn't reply. He simply turned and walked away.

"Where you going, Tommy?' Diaz demanded.

"To call this in," O'Meara replied, disgust in his tone. "Where's the fucking backup?"

"He shot at me once, Tommy. How the fuck did I know he wasn't turning to shoot again?"

15

An initial shooting inquest, whether the incident being investigated was clearly a justifiable use of force or not, was always a sober affair. Because a citizen had been killed under circumstances that were not altogether clear-cut, the mood at the 100th Street Manhattan North Borough Command that Tuesday afternoon was tense. Conflicting stories had circulated, some claiming the victim was unarmed. There was no question, in any account of events, that Oscar Delacruz, unemployed itinerant laborer, age twenty-three and a native of the Dominican Republic, had been shot twice in the back.

Tom O'Meara, seated alone in the inquest room hot seat, waited patiently for the shooting panel to convene behind a table, ten feet out in front of him. If he closed his eyes, he could still conjure a vivid image of that pathetic spark plugger, trembling on the sidewalk in a spreading pool of his own blood. He could conjure the look of surprise in the dying man's eyes, and the look of bewilderment in Eddie's expression.

The man who had the duty that afternoon in Manhattan North's Fifth Division, Captain John LaValle, was already seated at the table with the Fifth Division commanding officer, Deputy Inspector William Foxcroft. Both men were younger than O'Meara, LaValle by ten years, and Foxcroft not by much. Another dinosaur. They were easy in each other's company, and easy in Tom's. The sergeant was a grizzled veteran by any standard. They weren't any happier to see him before them than he was to be there.

The door opened and Deputy Chief Terrence Kelly entered the room. Patrol Borough Manhattan North's commanding officer, Kelly was a trim, silver-haired dynamo, resplendent in tailored blue and gold. The same age as O'Meara, they had attended the academy together. Tom was a street-smart cop while Kelly was what most rank-and-file policemen would describe as political. With a nod to his fellow brass, he crossed to shake hands with his old classmate.

"Sorry we couldn't make Morgan's party," he apologized. "I asked Mary Anne to send flowers."

"She got them," Tom replied. "They were beautiful. Thanks."

Kelly moved toward his seat at the table as Field Internal Affairs Unit Captain Frank Oliver entered.

"I think you know everyone here, don't you, Tommy?" Chief Kelly asked O'Meara.

Tom shifted in his chair to get more comfortable, and said he did. As much as he and most other cops hated the shooflies, he'd been to enough of these things over the years to know that somebody in Frank Oliver's capacity had to be there.

"I've got a community affairs liaison breathing down my neck about this, so let's make it short and sweet," Kelly told them.

Tom braced himself.

"You want to give it to us in your own words, Tommy? Exactly what happened?" Kelly asked.

Up to the point where O'Meara had seen that weapon fly from the fleeing perp's hand into the doorway of that building, he related events just as they had developed.

"Eddie had a good fifteen yards on me by the time he reached that intersection with Thayer Street," he continued from there. "A cab cut across, separating us for a second just as I saw the perp start to turn. After taking the fire the way he did, less than thirty seconds earlier, I'm sure my partner was pretty jacked up. I know I was. I'm sure he figured the man was gonna shoot at him again, and he discharged his weapon. I heard two shots. By the time I reached the opposite curb, Mr. Delacruz was on the pavement, that little nine millimeter he fired at us, on the ground under his right hip."

Chief Kelly regarded him with a steady, even stare. "We've had some conflicting eyewitness reports, Tommy. Two people are saying this Delacruz threw that gun away; that a cop fitting your description retrieved it from a doorway, then gave it to Diaz to plant on the man."

O'Meara stared straight back, and shrugged. "Bullshit, Terry. Eddie shot him in the back, granted. But he'd already been fired at twice at close range. I doubt I would've done it any differently than he did. It was one of those split-second decisions a cop hopes he'll never have to make."

Apparently satisfied, Chief Kelly nodded to a uniformed clerk seated beside a tape recorder. She turned it off.

"That's probably all we'll need from you, Tommy," Kelly said. "You okay with this?"

O'Meara took a deep breath and shrugged. Terry could have no idea how far removed from okay Tom was about any of it. That afternoon, he'd watched his partner gun down an unarmed man. He'd just lied about what he'd seen to one of his oldest and most influential friends on the job. Frankly, he felt like shit. "Yeah, I'm fine. Thanks."

"You call Sheila? Tell her about it yet?"

"Not yet. No. I guess I'd better, before she hears it on the news, huh?"

"Not a bad idea," Kelly agreed. "You need a lift back to the station house?"

Tom said he appreciated the offer, but that his car was parked right outside.

Ever since Tom O'Meara had disappeared behind the door to that shooting-inquest room, Eddie Diaz had been sitting on pins and needles. It was standard operating procedure that any cop who pulled the trigger in a shooting incident be given immediate counseling. Eddie had been forced to endure an hour and a half of psychological hugs and kisses from a well-meaning but ineffectual department shrink. Thank God his PBA rep showed up a half hour into the session, and helped ward off some of the worst of the counselor's touchy-feely palaver. By the time Diaz emerged from that ordeal, O'Meara had gone into the inquest. One of the cops in the hallway, Chief Kelly's driver, told him the Internal Affairs man had just put in an appearance twenty minutes ago. The PBA rep suggested Diaz go home and get some rest, but Eddie insisted he'd wait for his partner. The rep decided to wait with him. Fearful of wolves, Eddie supposed.

When the door to the inquest room opened, and Tom came through, Eddie didn't fail to notice how pale his partner looked. O'Meara saw him sitting there and locked eyes for a moment. Eddie felt a huge wave of relief wash over him. The sarge had stood up.

"Hey, Tommy," Eddie greeted him.

Deputy Chief Terrence Kelly emerged in O'Meara's wake. If Eddie wasn't mistaken, the chief had seen the look that went between him and his partner. His suspicion was confirmed when Chief Kelly looked directly at him.

"You're Diaz?"

"Yes, sir."

The PBA rep was on her feet in a flash. "I've informed Officer Diaz that he isn't required to make a statement for forty-eight hours, Chief Kelly."

Kelly gave her the cold eye. "I'm well aware of that policy, Ms. Hoffman. I helped write it." He then turned back to Diaz, and winked. "Take her advice, Office Diaz. From the way Sergeant O'Meara has described it, you've been through a traumatic experience. Go home and get some rest."

Kelly joined his driver and started for the door while Tom O'Meara retrieved his jacket from a nearby coat rack. Eddie left the PBA rep's side to hurry toward his partner.

"Officer Diaz," she called after him, the impatience clear in her tone.

"Later," he waved her off. "I appreciate what you did for me in there."

"Not a word, Eddie. Not to anyone," she warned. "They want a statement, you want me to be there."

Diaz grabbed his own jacket. By the time he caught up with his partner, the sarge was outside the front door and headed for their cruiser.

"How'd it go in there?" Eddie asked.

Tom's gaze was set on some unseen object in the distance. "Fine. You're in the clear." His voice was tight in his throat.

"I'm in the clear. What does that mean?"

Tom stopped dead in the middle of the sidewalk and spun. "You shot the bastard in the back, Eddie. Unarmed. Running away."

"I didn't know he'd tossed the gun, Tom. I swear to God I didn't."

O'Meara's glare had gone ice cold. "His bad luck I guess, huh, Eddie?"

Diaz threw his hands up in frustration. "What the fuck are you saying, boss? The motherfucker already took two shots at me. What was I supposed to think?"

"Crime Scene Unit found an empty gun case in that Beemer, Eddie. The dumb fuck probably found the damned thing in there. Figures it would be easier to turn for quick cash than the radio. He sees the cruiser, right on his ass, and he panics. Lets loose with a couple."

Diaz couldn't believe he was hearing this. "Hindsight's always twenty-twenty," he snapped. "You got your veins pumped full of adrenaline, sometimes things get a little fuzzy at the edges."

"In a potbellied pig's eye," O'Meara spat. "We're sworn to protect and serve, not to gun down unarmed citizens like this is fucking Tombstone, and you're Wyatt Earp."

Tom O'Meara had no idea how long he'd sat on that stool at the end of the first likely bar he could find, driving south from the station house through Morningside Heights. Halfway between Columbia University, just to the south of him, and City College, to the north, the establishment was one of those New York anomalies. Two blocks west of the heart of Harlem, it hardly had a black patron in it. Some of the clientele looked academic, but most of them looked blue-collar white. Where they'd come from and where they lived, Tom had no idea. In fact, right now, he had very few ideas about much of anything. He'd ordered his first Bushmills with a beer back a little after four-thirty. At seven o'clock, he'd handed the bartender a napkin with his home number on it and requested the man call Sheila, to tell her where he was.

When Rory Devaney climbed up onto the stool alongside O'Meara and asked the barkeep for a Harp lager, it took Tom a moment of squinting at him in the dim light to realize why he recognized that voice.

"Rory. Whuda fuck you doin' here?"

"Sheila said you've had a rough day," Devaney replied. "Asked me t' look in on y'."

"Where's she?" Tom asked, and struggled around to search the barroom behind him.

"By the looks o' you, the same place you should be. Home."

On and off, there were two Rory Devaneys seated beside O'Meara. Not a good sign. Even as drunk as he was, he knew that if the room started to spin on him, he was in real trouble. "You drive a car, 'n' stay on the right?" he asked

"I've got a better chance than you, I reckon." Devaney waved to the man on the duckboards. "What's he owe y'?" he asked.

When the bartender returned with the tab, Tom made a lame attempt to grab it. "Gimme that," he complained.

"I'll trade y' for the car keys," Rory suggested.

The impact of the cold November night air hitting him full in the face did O'Meara a world of good. He led Devaney up the block outside the bar to where he thought he'd parked his car, and sure enough, it was where he thought he'd left it. Wipers, tires, window glass, radio, and all. "I c'n prob'ly drive," he offered as Rory stopped to unlock the passenger-side door. "If you're not c'mf'table, drivin' in a big, strange city."

Devaney chuckled as he opened the door for him and stood aside. "Not bloody likely, mate. The only thing you'll be drivin' t'night is the porcelain bus."

Devaney got Tom strapped into the seat beside him, head lolling back against the rest and the stink of whisky so heavy that he had to run the windows down a crack. He then drove O'Meara's big Chrysler sedan south on the Belt Parkway, en route toward the Verrazano-Narrows Bridge. As they passed the lower end of Manhattan, with its bright-lit financial district and tightly clustered spires, it still awed him. All the film footage he'd seen of New York had never done the sheer bulk of what existed there, across the shining waters of the East River, anything approaching justice.

"Y' know what I can't get over about this city o' yours, Tom?" he asked aloud.

He'd thought O'Meara unconscious by now, and was surprised when he replied. "No. What?"

"The sheer scope of everything. It's like nobody ever told you people the world's got limits. I look at the Empire State Buildin', and try t' imagine what them builders was thinkin', way back in 1931. It's like they just put their minds t' the impossible, like the fookin' Incas or Egyptians, and there it stands. Done."

His eyes still closed, Tom smiled, albeit a bit stupidly, and nodded. "Yup."

"You feelin' all right there, Tom?"

O'Meara lifted his left hand to make the universal *OK* sign with thumb and forefinger. "Had a shootin', t'day. Eddie an' me. Guy stealin' radio from a car took a shot at us. Dumb shit panicked, I s'pose. Eddie killed 'im."

Sheila had mentioned something about a shooting, but none of the specifics. Rory had seen it on her face, just how often she'd thought about Tom leaving home some morning and never coming back. Rory knew all too well what those fears were like. His heart had gone out to her. "He shot a y' first, Tom. That makes him a bad guy. Here, or anywhere."

Slowly, O'Meara shook his head side to side. "Not bad, jus' stupid. Threw the gun away, but Eddie didn't see. Couple punk arrests was all he had on his sheet."

O'Meara suddenly sat up straighter in his seat and started grabbing for his seat belt release. "Pull over!"

Rory saw the way his passenger's eyes bulged, and steered for the beltway guardrail. It was another hundred yards before he could find a little emergency turnout and brake to stop. By then, Tom had his door open and was struggling to lean his head out of the car. Once they stopped, O'Meara tumbled out onto his hands and knees to retch.

For a good ten minutes, Devaney sat where he was behind the wheel and watched the steady stream of late commuter traffic roll past. He knew what this sort of a drunk was all about, and had embarked on more than a few of them himself, when matters had turned particularly ugly. Once Tom finished puking his guts out, he took a moment outside the car to collect himself. After he climbed back in, both of them stared straight ahead into the night for a long moment, without speaking.

"Gonna be okay, mate?"

"Gimme a minute."

"Ask y' a personal question?" Rory ventured.

O'Meara shrugged. "You've seen me on my hands and knees puking. What's personal anymore?"

"Y' ever shoot anyone? Yourself, I mean."

O'Meara looked over at him, frowning. "Why you ask?"

"I see how hard you're takin' this. It's just a question."

O'Meara stared back out into the night. "In thirty years, I've drawn my service weapon exactly four times. And no. Thank God, I've never actually had to shoot anybody with it."

"Y' pick up a gun, sooner or later, someone gets a bullet," Rory murmured.

Tom looked sharply in his direction. "What was that?"

Rory reached to ease the shift lever into drive again. "Big boys' rules."

O'Meara shifted slightly in his seat to face him, most of the earlier signs of drunkenness vanished. "What the hell do you know about big boys' rules?"

Devaney shrugged. "I'm from Belfast, remember. They're fairly common knowledge, I suppose."

Tom's eyes narrowed as he continued to stare at Rory. "So let me ask you a personal question."

"Turnabout's fair," Rory agreed.

"There's a war of sorts going on in Belfast. You ever shoot anybody?"

Rory steered them back into traffic, and drove deep in thought for a while. "At dinner one night, when I was eight, masked men broke into our house and killed my da."

They rode the rest of the way to the O'Meara house on Staten Island in silence. It wasn't until Rory pulled the car into the drive and removed the key from the ignition that Tom finally spoke. In the dark, the lights extinguished, he reached to pat Devaney on the shoulder.

"I'm sorry about your father, Rory. I can't imagine what it had to be like for you."

Devaney breathed deep, those vivid memories evoked by the smell of incense that past Saturday flooding back. "Be thankful, Tom."

"They ever catch the fuckers who did it?"

Rory couldn't help but smile. Tom was a policeman. In his world, policemen hunted murderers down and brought them to justice. "Y' mean, was there a happy endin'? No, Tom. It's an Irish story, not an American one. In Ireland, there are no happy endings."

16

◆

A badly hungover Tom O'Meara did something Wednesday morning that he'd done only a handful of times in his entire thirty years on the job. He called in sick. With Sheila and Rory gone off to work, and the girls off to school, he spent the morning trying to get a perspective on what had happened yesterday. He believed in his heart that Eddie Diaz had made an honest mistake. But in any other walk of life, if you made a mistake that cost a man his life, honest or not, there was generally a price to pay. That was why doctors had malpractice insurance. Tom had lied for Eddie because he liked him, because he was his partner, and because a cop never knew when he might find himself in the same deep shit. Still, as he consumed close to a gallon of seltzer water mixed with orange juice, two packets of

Di-Gel, and a double dose of ibuprofen, Tom just couldn't get the decision he'd made to sit right.

Wednesdays, Chief Terry Kelly taught a class on arrest procedure to new recruits at the Police Academy on East Twentieth Street in Manhattan. Early that afternoon, not knowing exactly why, Tom found himself headed in that direction. He decided to leave his car behind and take public transportation, realizing it was years since he'd last ridden to Manhattan on the ferry. Born in the Bay Ridge section of Brooklyn, a graduate of Erasmus Hall High School and the City College of New York, O'Meara had lived in this city all his life. As he rode the Staten Island Rapid Transit Railway to St. George Station, and then stood along the starboard bow rail of the ferry, he stared out at this city that was his, and wondered what it would feel like to leave it. He'd read a book by Lawrence Block once where Block claimed that every human being had a spiritual home. Not necessarily the place of his birth, but the place where his soul felt grounded. Tom had traveled in his life, to Vietnam and Turkey in the service. He'd gone with Sheila to Dublin, London, and Paris on vacations, but nowhere felt like this place did to him. New York was in his blood, and yet, it might well be his spiritual home, too.

Terry Kelly was located in one of the Academy's second-floor lecture halls, resplendent in his starched and creased chief's rig before a host of bright-eyed, eager recruits. O'Meara slid along one wall and eased into an empty desk chair toward the back of the room and was reminded, yet again, of just how much the job had changed since 1966. Better than one quarter of this class was female. At least a third was Hispanic or black. A few of them were big, the way all cops had to be back when Tom signed on.

"Remember," Kelly was telling them. "Making the collar is only half your task. Making it stick's the other half, and that's usually when the hard work begins. This isn't *Kojak* or *Starsky and Hutch*. Each time we make a bust, we've got a constitution and court of law to answer to. You sweat the details and always think about how it'll play before a judge, and you'll be an effective police officer, guaranteed."

The class was scheduled to end in a few minutes when O'Meara entered the room. This had to be the wrap-up. Around the lecture hall, recruits were sneaking glances at the clock, many of them with their notebooks already closed.

"Next Wednesday, we'll review Patrol Guide booking procedure, step-by-step. Not sexy stuff, but by the time you leave this class in June, you'll know it in your sleep. Thank you, ladies and gentlemen. You're dismissed."

Kelly had seen O'Meara enter the hall. Once he answered a half-dozen questions, he left the podium to start in his old classmate's direction.

"Tommy," he greeted O'Meara. They shook hands.

"Brave new world," Tom commented as the class streamed out the lecture hall doors.

"You know it." Kelly lowered his voice. "It's the lardasses I just can't abide. The right to be fat in a job that requires mobility; the ability to respond appropriately in times of crisis? That's taking this P.C. bullshit too far."

O'Meara thought of Ignacio Gomez and grunted. Twice in a week, Gomez had left his partner's backside unprotected, simply because he was unable to give adequate chase. "Got time for a cup of coffee?" he asked.

Terry grinned. "Your timing's perfect. I'm headed to the cafeteria. You had lunch?"

The thought of food made O'Meara's guts do a back flip. "Called in with a touch of the Bushmills flu this morning," he admitted. "Don't think I'm quite ready for solid food, yet."

Terry clapped him on the shoulder. "Understood. I hope the sight of it won't bother you too much. I didn't have breakfast. I'm starving."

It was interesting to watch the kind of swath a deputy chief cut in an environment like that one. O'Meara had always had an aversion to the political end of the job, preferring, once he made sergeant, to forgo any further climb up the command ladder. Kelly, on the other hand, had always been marked for this sort of rise. He was a cocksure academy recruit, a savvy, ambitious patrolman, and had shot up through the ranks like a meteor. Today, he wore his uniform the way a chief should, projecting just the right mix of absolute self-confidence, controlled accessibility, and love for his work. Not a soul ignored the fact of his presence, everywhere he walked.

In the cafeteria, O'Meara got himself a cup of black coffee, and another glass of juice. He followed Kelly to a table in one corner where Terry, always conscious of his weight, sat down to a green salad, and a turkey sandwich.

"I had a peek at your driver's file," Kelly said. He toyed with the lettuce of his salad with his fork. "You know he's got two other shootings in that folder?"

Tom nodded. "One in Bed Stuy, his second year. The other in Chinatown, in the middle of a gang war. That time, him and six other cops all pulled their weapons. Eddie's a good cop, Terry."

"A bleeding-heart prosecutor at the D.A.'s office wants to believe one of those two eyewitnesses, Tommy. Says the lady's credible. She swears your dead guy threw his gun away."

O'Meara stared hard at his old friend. "It's her word against ours, Terry. When the ballistics tests come back, they won't dispute the fact the mutt fired at us. Twice."

Kelly held up a hand to stop him. "I'm not asking you to change your story, Tommy. I'm just informing you of what kinda trouble might lie ahead. The D.A. decides to take this to a grand jury, it could get a little ugly for you. Not that I don't think you'll come out of it all right. Still, no cop wants to be put on the fucking griddle like that."

"The mutt shot at cops," O'Meara reiterated.

"Fact. What grand jury's gonna prosecute a case like that?"

"That's why you'll walk away, if it ever goes that far. But if it does, just watch. You think you know who your friends are in this job. Then someone tries to smear shit on you, and everybody runs, afraid some of that stink might rub off on them."

When Sheila O'Meara got the call from Tom, mid-afternoon, he'd asked if she could find a half hour or so, break away and meet him at a diner a few blocks from her office on Arden Avenue. She arrived there to find her husband already seated in one of the booths. The usual lunch crowd had cleared out, and several of the middle-aged waitresses were on stools at the counter, resting weary feet. Tom looked haggard. He half rose as she slid onto the opposite bench and leaned over to kiss her cheek.

"How you feeling?" she asked.

"Probably better than I look," he admitted. "Sorry about last night, Sheel. Don't quite know what got into me."

She reached across the table and took one of his big, tough-guy hands in hers. "I think I do," she said softly. "You ran what happened back and forth so many times in your mind, trying to see a way you might have done it differently, that it started to make you crazy. Another part of you figured, drown it in alcohol and maybe it'll stay drowned."

He sucked at his teeth, then pursed his lips and nodded. "Sometimes it scares me, how well you know me. Hungry?"

"I had lunch, thanks. What about you? Have you eaten anything today?"

"Didn't think I could," he admitted, "Until just now. I ordered a piece of banana cream pie, of all things."

"Your blood sugar's low." She figured she'd better fix pasta that night for dinner. The next thing he would start to crave was carbohydrates. Her father was a binge drinker, and when he came off one, he was so hopelessly predictable it had become a kind of pathetic joke around her house.

"I went to see Terry Kelly," Tom told her. "He was teaching a class at the academy today. Tells me there's some assistant D.A. with a wild hair up his ass; that there's a chance they might take this to a grand jury."

She moaned. Several years back, one of Tom's closest friends, then a uniformed patrol lieutenant at the Tenth Precinct in Manhattan, was involved in a shooting that ultimately wound up before a grand jury. Half of the cops who he'd thought were his friends couldn't run away from him fast enough. The tabloids in the city had a field day, portraying him and his partner as virtual storm troopers. Then a witness came forward. He testified he'd seen the man they'd shot, a gun in his hand and taking aim.

Tom's slice of pie arrived. He offered her a bite and she shook her head no. After Morgan's confirmation party she'd gotten on the scale, shocked to see she'd gained two pounds last weekend. No pie or anything else fattening for her until those two pounds came off.

He took his first bite, expression thoughtful, then looked deep into her eyes. "The mutt Eddie shot didn't have a gun in his hand, Sheel. He tossed it while he was fleeing."

She blinked. "What?"

"The asshole had taken two shots at him and Eddie was pretty jacked up. He swears he didn't see Delacruz throw the gun away. When the kid stopped all of a sudden and started to turn, he thought it was to take another crack at him."

"Holy Mother. So you covered for him?"

Tom nodded. "When the mutt tossed the gun, I stopped to pick it up. The D.A. has a witness."

Sheila was speechless.

"Terry agrees that it's our word against hers," he continued. "Once they get the facts, he doubts the grand jury will even agree to hear it."

"And that's it?" she asked, an understandable dubiousness in her tone.

He shook his head. "I've decided, it goes to a grand jury, I can't sit up there on the stand and call this witness a goddamn liar. Before I do that, I'll throw in my papers. The way this knee's been bugging me lately, it might be time to go, anyway."

It was something she'd been afraid to beg him to do for the last ten years. Now, she couldn't believe she was hearing it. She squeezed his hand. "Nobody wants you off the street more than I do, baby. But not like this. That job is your whole life. For thirty years, you never took money, never used your tin to throw your weight around, never treated anyone unfairly, no matter who or what they were. A cop with a record like that walks away with his head held high."

Tom closed his eyes. "He was stealing a radio, for crissakes. He didn't deserve to get killed for stealing a radio, Sheel."

She squeezed again and kept the pressure on this time. "Eddie made the mistake. Not you. And there's not a cop on the street who wouldn't forgive him for it."

Tom removed his hand from hers, pushed the half-eaten pie away, and collapsed back against the banquette. "Maybe not, Sheel. And maybe that's what my problem is. Yesterday morning on the way into work, I still loved the idea of being a street cop. Today, I just don't have the stomach for it anymore."

It took her a long moment to adjust to this sudden turn their lives had taken. To hell with her diet. She picked up his fork and scooped up a big bite of banana cream. "I never told you this," she said as she savored how that sweetness filled her mouth. Damn, they made great pies here. "But I was probably the only Irish girl in Brooklyn who didn't want to marry a cop or a fireman."

"You could've saved yourself a lot of pain, you'd just said no when I asked."

"But I didn't marry a cop," she insisted. "I fell in love with a man who just happened to be one. I'm still in love with him, and whoever he decides to be, next."

* * *

It was times like this that Tom O'Meara understood why, in a world where more than half of all marriages failed, his hadn't. For twenty-three years, his wife had also been his best friend. Often times, she understood who he was and what motivated him better than he did, himself. Besides, twenty-three years, three kids, and uncounted sleepless nights worrying about him later, she was more beautiful and sexy today than she was when she agreed to be his bride. In her car, as she drove him back to the house, he studied that profile with its high forehead, pert, upturned nose, and bright, intelligent blue eyes.

"With you still a rising star in the world of real estate, it won't be long before I go stir-crazy, rattling around that empty house all by myself."

A slow smile spread from the corners of her mouth and eyes. "Maybe we should break you in gently."

At least on occasion, she wasn't the only one who could read minds. "How's that?" he asked, playing along.

"I was just thinking. The girls won't be home from school for another hour and a half. And I didn't really want to go back to the office."

"Ah," he said. "Gently, you say?"

Her smile broke wide now. "Maybe not that gently. But if you behave, I promise I won't hurt you."

Tom didn't give a damn which of his neighbors

was home in the middle of the day and looking out their windows as he hurried from the car to follow Sheila to the front porch. He caught her from behind as she sorted through her ring for the house key, turned her and kissed her hard. Rather than resist, she eased all her lithe, womanly warmth up against him and ground her hips, their tongues playing tag. Once they finally broke their kiss off, he touched his forehead to hers and rubbed noses.

"How long has it been since I told you how beautiful you are, and how much I love you?" he asked.

"Not since last night. But you were so drunk, I wasn't sure I should believe you."

He reached to slap her ass. "Well I'm not drunk now," he growled.

She ground her hips against him again, and chuckled. "Clearly. Either you let me open the door, Tom O'Meara, or be prepared to take me right here, before God and all our neighbors as witnesses."

He frowned. "I believe that would be breaking the law."

"You're retiring. Get over it."

"Besides being in fairly poor taste."

She pulled her head back. "Good point. Let me open the door."

17

◆

After thirty years on the job, Tom O'Meara had developed a sort of sixth sense about danger. The moment Sheila opened the front door and stepped into the house ahead of him, he could sense that someone was inside, and looking at them. Maybe he was tipped by a glimpsed shadow. Perhaps he'd heard a faint noise that was different from the rumble of the furnace or the slight squeal of the front door hinge. His reactions were instinctive by now. One moment Sheila strode purposefully ahead of him across the front room, stripping out of her coat, and the next he raced forward to grab her. Before he had an opportunity to explain, the situation explained itself.

From a corner of the room near Tom's favorite chair, a masked man leapt up like a jack-in-the-box and bolted for the kitchen. O'Meara's right knee screamed as he spun to give chase.

"Call the cops!" he snapped.

The pain in his knee be damned, Tom was halfway through the hall toward the kitchen when he heard the back door slam open and the sound of fleeing footsteps on the back porch. He was so riveted on the man he pursued that he failed to see another leap out from the stairs to the basement and tackle him. Together, they went down hard, with Tom able to use momentum in his favor. As they landed on the hallway floor, he drove a shoulder into his attacker's solar plexus and continued on over the top of him. He landed upright on his knees, stunned but not incapacitated, while his taller, more wiry opponent struggled to rise. O'Meara brought a fist up from down low and caught the masked man flush on the side of the face. That sent him reeling backward as O'Meara clawed at his ankle trying to clear his off-duty weapon from his holster.

From the living room, Tom could hear Sheila shouting into the telephone. "Ten-thirteen! Ten-thirteen! Officer in trouble! Six-three-two Hammock Lane! Hurry, please!"

Tom managed to get his weapon cleared just as his masked attacker was shaking off that blow to the head. The man could take one hell of a punch, and as soon as he saw that gun in O'Meara's hand, he reacted like the sight was smelling salts. Tom was fumbling for the safety on the compact Smith & Wesson automatic when the downed man leapt to his feet and came at him.

* * *

Sheila O'Meara looked on helplessly from the living room, the receiver still in her hand, as Tom and his attacker careened off a wall, grappling for the little gun. An instant later they disappeared from view in the direction of a window overlooking the side yard, and she heard the crash of shattered glass. Tom kept his service weapon in a locked gun safe in the bedroom closet. The key was in his top dresser drawer. There was nothing she could think of to help him right now except to run and try to get it, hoping she returned in time. Good God. This was madness. Her husband was a thirty-year veteran of the New York PD. This wasn't supposed to happen to people like them.

Sheila was turning to set the receiver back in its cradle and run for the stairs when the front door, still slightly ajar, flew open. That first masked man reentered the house to come at her. With a scream, she swung the phone at his head.

The instant Tom saw that he and his opponent were about to hit glass, he gave up trying to retain possession of his gun. He quit fighting and used the other man's resistance to help ditch the weapon out of reach. One minute the guy was fighting him for it. The next instant he had possession, but his hand and arm were also outside the house, along with a hail of broken glass. His surprise, coupled with his fear of being cut to shreds, gave Tom an opening to square up and knee him in the groin. His opponent doubled up, sagging to his knees, choking, and got clubbed in the head with an elbow for good measure. O'Meara was straightening, trying to catch his breath, when Sheila screamed.

The door in the living room now flung wide, a second masked man had his back to Tom, a flailing Sheila clutched in a choke hold. She had the receiver of the phone in one hand and was swinging it wildly.

Tom leapt into the fray, fists flying. He hammered hard at the man's kidneys, forcing him to let Sheila go to defend himself. The moment he did, Tom kicked his feet from beneath him and jammed that bad knee into the middle of the man's back to drive him to the floor.

"Get out!" he yelled at Sheila. "Go! Run!"

In her panic, she ran for the kitchen, rather than the front door, and smack into Tom's first opponent. Staggering but able to gather himself, the guy came at her from a crouch and knocked her flat on her back. With one more staggering step he was on O'Meara again. Now it was two-to-one, and Tom got a nasty sinking feeling about his odds.

Rory Devaney had spent most of the morning with Megan Desmond, traveling by subway to meet her and purchase round-trip plane fare to Dublin. They'd then returned to the tug to go over the detailed itinerary she would follow, one more time. Just to be with her as much as anything else, he'd accompanied her back to Manhattan that afternoon.

They'd spent an hour together drinking beer and talking in a bar a block from the Fitzsimmons house, on West Tenth Street. It was three o'clock before he got back aboard a Number One train to South Ferry, and managed to run and catch the next boat to St. George station. En route back to the O'Meara house, he wondered how Sean was getting on with his surveillance of Billy Burke, and wondered how Tom was getting on with his hangover. He also fretted over the panicked look he'd seen on Judge Pete Fitzsimmons's face when he dropped Megan back at the town house. The man had looked like a trapped and frightened animal. Fleeing upstairs as soon as he realized it was Rory with Megan, he didn't look much like an ardent Irish patriot, out busting his arse to raise that last million dollars Rory needed to seal his deal. Not that such a reaction was unexpected. Rory had become an expert at gauging how fear could eat at a man's courage. He'd early on suspected the judge to be deficient in that area. It was why he'd set Sean to following Billy Burke. The good St. Burke would be remembered as a patron of the Provisional IRA whether he agreed to part with those Stingers for money or was forced to surrender them at gunpoint. After all, this *was* war.

Thus preoccupied, Devaney was halfway up the front walk toward the O'Mearas' front porch when he noticed both Tom's and Sheila's cars were parked in the drive. She didn't generally get home from the office until five or after. Tom had probably called in sick today, but both of them home? Having it off before the kiddies returned from school perhaps. Rory turned, ready to trot off to Tiny's Tavern when he heard Sheila scream, a man bellow, and then a crash. It was then that he realized the front door was open on a day when temperatures were running in the low thirties.

The handiest object Rory could grab as a weapon was a length of split maple from a small stack of firewood kept in a bin to the left of the veranda. He hefted it to find its balance point and charged ahead through the open front door.

"Go on! Run, baby!" Tom was shouting to Sheila as he struggled with two masked men on the living room floor. Back near the archway toward the central hallway and kitchen, Sheila was on her hands and knees, scrambling to find her feet. Clearly torn as to whether she should try to help her husband or run, she seemed paralyzed with indecision.

"Go!" Rory yelled at her as he leapt into the fray. With his first swing, he caught one of Tom's attackers across the shoulders with that chunk of firewood, staggering him. On the backswing, he clobbered the other opponent in the head and then skipped back a quick step to drive an instep into the man's rib cage. The first one he'd clobbered was hard to keep down. He absorbed the blow with a confused shake of the head, and came up at Rory with too much determination. Rather than swing the log and risk the bigger man taking it away from him, Rory threw it to distract him, then dropped to the floor and drove a heel up hard into his groin. By that time, Tom was on the first guy and making sure he stayed down. Rory's opponent collapsed in a heap as the Irishman retrieved that chunk of maple. He drew back for the coup de grâce, determined to split the bastard's head like a melon, when a shadow of movement caught his attention.

"Do it and I blow her fuckin' head off," a voice snarled.

Both Rory and Tom froze. They turned to see a third masked man in the kitchen doorway, one arm hugging Sheila close and a sawed-off shotgun jammed under her chin.

"Jesus!" O'Meara gasped.

"Tom?" Sheila whispered, her voice quavering with terror.

"Let 'em up," the gunman snapped. "Now!"

Slowly, both Rory and O'Meara backed away from their opponents.

"Take it easy," Tom said softly as he moved. "We'll do exactly as you say."

"Both of youse, back against the wall," the gunman ordered.

They moved to comply, Tom still talking in that same, calm negotiator's voice. "Whatever you want, take it. There's no problem."

"Shut the fuck up!" the gunman snarled. "C'mon, you assholes," he snapped at his cohorts. "Move!" And then he froze, the wail of a siren growing louder in the distance.

"He's a fucking cop!" one of the other two complained. "We gotta get outta here."

Rory watched the gunman and Tom O'Meara lock eyes.

Tom spoke again with that same spooky calm. "Once they get here, it gets a whole lot more complicated. Right now you can still walk away."

A war of wills was waged for another few seconds. It seemed to Rory like an eternity. Then the gunman's grip tightened on Sheila as he started back into the kitchen. "You fuckin' sneeze, you're scraping brains off the ceiling, motherfucker," he rasped.

That single wail of a siren had split and was now two, both units coming fast. Once his pals were clear, the gunman shoved Sheila back into the hallway and disappeared behind the kitchen door. She stumbled two steps, trying to catch her balance, then ran and threw herself into her husband's arms.

"Don't chase them, please," she begged, sobbing with relief.

"Don't worry, baby," he crooned, stroking her hair. "They're gone. It's over. We're okay. Everything is all right."

It wasn't until they heard the screech of braking tires and whump of closed car doors that any of them moved. Tom, clearly shaken, then eased away from his wife and started for the front door.

Sheila wiped her eyes and looked at Rory. It was then that he realized he still gripped that chunk of firewood.

"You okay?" she whispered.

"Fine," he said. "And you?"

"I don't think I've ever been so frightened in my life."

With both barrels of a sawed-off twelve gauge ready to blow her brains out, he couldn't blame her. That was as close as anyone ever came to it, and still walked away.

A dozen cops combed the house and yard while two plainclothes detectives from Staten Island's 123rd Precinct took the O'Mearas' statements. Rory excused himself to head for the basement on the pretense of retrieving his passport, and the first thing he did, once he locked the bathroom door behind him, was push aside the clothes hamper and make sure his cache was intact. There was no question in his mind what those three had been after, and inside he was boiling with barely controlled rage. Billy Burke, realizing that the wheels were coming off the Provo's latest offensive effort, had decided to have his cake and eat it, too. Why take less for a shipment of missiles than he knew he could get elsewhere, when he could take the IRA's money, anyway? St. Burke, patron of the cause, champion of martyrs, widows, and orphans.

The money was still in its hidey-hole, but how long it might stay there was anyone's guess. Because he could imagine no other way, at least at first thought, that Burke could have located him here, he remonstrated himself for getting sloppy. And then he thought on, his mind racing over other possibilities, a mile a second. He thought of the look he'd seen that afternoon on Judge Pete Fitzsimmons's face. As soon as he could slip away from here, he had to make contact with Sean, to warn him to be careful. If Fitzsimmons was seeking to erase any trace of his IRA connections, what better way to do it than sell both Rory and Sean Geary out to Burke? And what easier way than for the lordly sum of two million dollars?

To hell with worrying about hangovers. Tom O'Meara mixed both him and his wife tall tumblers of Bushmills and water over ice. While Sheila gave her statement to the two detectives in the dining room, Tom stood at the kitchen sink and stared out at those uniforms still combing his yard. So far as anyone could determine, nothing in the house was missing. Not jewelry, not a single item from Tom's valuable baseball card collection, not a stereo, television, or even the baseball atop his dresser bearing signatures of the entire 1961 New York Yankees World Series Championship team. What kind of thug who said "youse" and "motherfucker" could pass up a trophy like that? O'Meara had a cop's suspicious mind, tempered by thirty years of unlikely coincidences. Stupid mutts did predictably stupid things, and most everything sooner or later added up. But something here was way out of whack. There was no doubt in his mind that those three were after something here, and it wasn't money to score dope. Pipeheads who broke into houses rarely worked in teams. And he was damned sure he'd never busted one, let alone three, all wearing ski masks.

18

◆

Convinced that the last time he was in Burke's Bar his comings and goings had been monitored via some sort of surveillance system, Rory Devaney had spent time on a bar stool searching the ornate mahogany woodwork for a camera. He'd finally located a little convex dome of glass, perhaps one inch in diameter, set directly above the center of the back-bar mirror. To a casual observer it might look like ornamentation of some sort, but not to Rory. It was a camera lens.

Rush hour in Manhattan was winding down, but this was matinee day on Broadway. A combination of the regular after-work crowd and Broadway stragglers jammed Burke's barroom to near capacity. Rory imagined that in a crowd such as this, his arrival might go unnoticed in the office upstairs. To ensure that it didn't, he stopped directly before that surveillance camera, looked up, and waved.

He then walked through to the dining room, past the several dozen evening theatergoers eating early suppers, and mounted the stairs.

Billy Burke was staring directly at the door when Rory opened it to walk in. Calm as a statue of the serene, sitting Buddha, he merely nodded as Rory eased past a pair of men in familiar black sweaters and trousers. Once he sat on the sofa, he and Burke stared at each other for a long moment. It was Rory who finally spoke.

"Just what is it y' think you're doin', Billy?"

Burke continued to stare at him but failed to reply. Rory glanced around the room and noticed that one of the two goons had several nasty bruises on his face. "I bet this room is pretty well insulated, i'nt it? So's y' can conduct your more, ah, delicate affairs in privacy." He could see the sound-deadening material screwed to the back of the door and had earlier noticed the sort of egg-carton foam material used in recording studios glued to the ceiling. Without warning, he whipped his 9-mm pistol from inside his jacket and shot the thug with the bruised face in his left knee. The man howled and fell to the carpet, the deep beige pile splashed now with bright dabs of crimson.

"Get him out of here," Burke snarled to the other thug. "Take the back stairs. Now!"

All the while, Billy's eyes never left Rory's. Slowly, Devaney eased his weapon back out of sight, one hand still on it.

"You're a stupid man, Mr. Burke. T' think that's my money y' tried t' steal. Until y' give me missiles for it, there's a thousand soldiers just like me who own it. All part of an army y' don't want as your enemy."

"You finished?" Burke asked, still as calm and serene as that statue.

"I'm wonderin' if I've managed t' penetrate at all, Billy. T' get y' to understand this in't a war y' want to start."

Burke finally moved. He folded his arms over his chest and shrugged. "Maybe you'll want to talk this over with your pal, Sean, before you go making any more assumptions about your power base . . . Frankie."

Devaney stiffened. "Perhaps I'll give him a call," he murmured.

"I'm afraid you wouldn't find him home," Burke replied. "But if you'd like to speak to him directly, I can probably arrange it."

When Rory didn't respond, his face frozen in a mask of fury, Burke smiled. "I think I know how much he'd like to see you. Seeing as you're comrades, and such old friends and all."

The rear of the building that housed Burke's Bar faced an alley wide enough to hold garbage Dumpsters and a parked car. Burke unlocked the gate at one end, swung it wide and drove his late model Lexus sedan out to collect Rory, standing on the sidewalk. Before he left, he hopped out of the car to secure that gate again. The ride that Devaney endured in silence was a short one, to a stretch of West Forty-fifth Street between Tenth and Eleventh Avenues. Burke pulled up adjacent to a gap between old warehouse buildings and tenements, where a railroad cut ran north and south below the surface of the street. He climbed out of the car to lead Rory to a commuter bus–washing facility just west of that forty-foot-deep cut in the midtown granite.

"You need to try and look at this the way I do, Mr. McGuire," Burke said as they proceeded up a wide, darkened driveway. "I'm a businessman, plain and simple. If money goes out, money's gotta come in. To cover it. If more money goes out than comes in, I'm no longer in business. We had a deal. You announced to me this morning that you can't hold up your end. Meanwhile, I'm out some serious cash."

They approached a car parked facing the street. Behind it stood a big, tunnellike structure, the back end of a bus visible inside. When Burke waved, his goon Teddy climbed out from behind the wheel to stand there in shadow.

"Where's Sean?" Rory growled.

"Patience," Burke replied. He held out his hand and Teddy placed a car key in it. Both men then led the way around to the trunk, where Burke fit the key into the lock. When he turned it and lifted the lid, the light inside the trunk came on. Sean Geary was revealed, gagged and trussed with duct tape, and clearly terrified.

His dry rage suddenly sparked to flame, Rory moved to pull his pistol. He had it halfway out of his jacket when Burke's hand came up, a tiny two-shot .45 caliber derringer aimed at the center of his forehead.

"Easy," Billy crooned. He nodded to Teddy.

The goon stepped forward to jerk Sean around, facedown, and reveal his bound hands. Both were bright red with blood. One was clearly mangled, with two fingers missing.

His gun still trained on Rory, Burke reached with his free hand to slam the trunk closed again. "Go get your pathetic army's money, Frankie. Two-thirds payment only buys you two thirds of the shipment. But some would be better than none, and I won't be out so much cash."

Teddy swung on Rory from his blind side, a short length of iron pipe connecting with the small of his back. It sent him sprawling.

Burke leaned down. "There's a warehouse on the northwest side of Greenwich Street. Between Gansevoort and Horatio," he growled. "Midnight, Frankie. You fuck with me, your friend there is dead."

To make sure Rory stayed down, Billy drew a foot back and kicked him hard in the ribs. As Rory folded up, gagging, Burke turned and sauntered back down the drive to his Lexus.

Sheila's car was packed with overnight bags for her and the girls. While Morgan and Annie sat in the backseat, Annie sniffling about having to leave her kitty behind, Bridget sat next to her mother up front. Tom O'Meara stood outside the driver's window and leaned down to kiss his wife good-bye. Their spontaneous plans for an afternoon roll in the hay long since forgotten, they were doing the only sensible thing. Tom was convinced the three thugs who'd invaded their lives were professionals. Having witnessed the one shove that shotgun up under Sheila's jaw, he was certain that until he got to the bottom of whatever this was, 632 Hammock Lane was off-limits to his precious family.

"Call me when you get to your sister's," he said. "Love you, baby." Moving on to the backseat, he reached in to wipe a tear from Annie's face with a thumb. "Fluffer's gonna be just fine, honey. I promise. Don't worry about him. I need you to take good care of Mommy."

A moment later, Tom stood in the drive watching the taillights of Sheila's car disappear around the corner, headed for Brooklyn. With Thanksgiving only a week away, it had turned bitter cold. His hands shoved deep into the pockets of his jacket, he hurried back toward the house with plenty on his mind. The computer in the den, three televisions, an expensive stereo, his card collection and a five-hundred-dollar watch in Sheila's jewelry box were untouched, all evidence pointing to some other object of interest. Something of which Tom was unaware. To send in a team of burglars, masked and armed, suggested to O'Meara that the prize they sought was significant.

Yes, Rory Devaney had come to the rescue. He had very probably turned the tide of battle that afternoon. And yes, Tom, Sheila, and all the rest of the family had become very fond of the Irishman. But the one question O'Meara had to ask himself was how well did they really know this guy. Ostensibly some distant relative of Pete Fitzsimmons, he'd come into their lives a total stranger.

Once inside the house again, Tom headed directly for the basement. When men broke into your home and one of them held a gun to your wife's head, it changed all the rules. If he found nothing in a search of Rory's belongings, and his guest later took offense at this display of mistrust, so be it. Tom had a responsibility that ran deeper than mere hospitality.

Twenty minutes into his basement search, conducted with all the crisp efficiency of a thirty-year police veteran, Tom moved on to the bathroom. Thus far, he'd found nothing more out of the ordinary in Rory's belongings than his passport, declaring him to be just who he said he was, and a Polaroid photograph of what looked like the inside of a boat cabin. Rory was in the arms of a very pretty young woman, and neither of them looked like they expected to have their picture taken.

The medicine cabinet contained all the usual toilet articles. There were no shaving cream cans with false bottoms, or toothpaste tubes with secreted uncut gemstones. Once Tom lifted the tank cover on the toilet to find only the brick he'd placed in it during a drought two years ago, he was ready to give up and move on. Then, as he turned to leave, he spotted the clothes hamper. When he hoisted it to dump its contents out onto the floor, a loose floor tile rattled. O'Meara froze.

Looking to save a little money when they'd renovated the basement and put in this bath, Tom had purchased a book on tile work. He'd done the floor, half-walls, and tub enclosure himself, and a damned fine job it was, if anyone cared to ask. The floor went down first, with him cutting one corner he probably shouldn't have. Rather than lay additional subflooring, he'd run mastic straight over the existing subfloor planking and glued those one-foot-by-one-foot ceramic tiles in place. The shortcut notwithstanding, the floor had stood up well to six years of drunken parties in Tom's basement bar. If none of the more heavily trafficked tiles in the middle of the bath had worked loose, there was surely no reason why two tiles along one wall, with the clothes hamper placed coincidentally atop them, should have. Two tiles, with the grout between them missing.

On his knees, O'Meara quickly lifted those two tiles to discover the subfloor beneath had been cut through, three pieces of planking, run on the diagonal, loose to the touch. In the hole to the subbasement crawl space beneath, Tom discovered a musty knapsack. It was stuffed full of loose, bulky objects, and it took a moment to get through the opening. Tom set it on the floor before him, and once the bag was unzipped, his heart nearly stopped. Those loose, bulky objects were banded stacks of one hundred dollar bills. Fifty to a stack. Five thousand dollars each. There had to be two or three hundred of them. Maybe more.

He used the phone on the little basement bar to try Deputy Chief Terrence Kelly at his home number. When he learned from Terry's teenage son that the chief was off at some Emerald Society function, Tom placed his next call to Eddie Diaz.

"Sarge," Diaz answered. "What's up?"

"No time to explain, Eddie. I'm at home. I need you here, quick as you can make it."

Diaz lived in Borough Park, Brooklyn, just a stone's throw from Ft. Hamilton Parkway. Once on it, he had a straight run of no more than ten minutes to the Verrazano-Narrows. If traffic was as light as it should be that time of night, Tom figured the trip might take him thirty minutes. Tops. Eddie told him to hang tight, he was already out the door.

So blind with rage that he could barely see straight anymore, Rory Devaney was now in a race against the clock. It was almost seven-thirty when Billy Burke left him gagging on his hands and knees on that Hell's Kitchen side street. With fifty-three dollars and change in his pockets, he'd debated taking a taxi back to Staten Island, then decided he could get as far as St. George Station faster by subway and ferry. By the time he reached Staten Island and hailed a cab outside the ferry terminal, it was quarter past eight. He wouldn't have his hands on

Burke's money until at least nine o'clock, which still left him three hours to make his Greenwich Village rendezvous. Plenty of time.

Sheila's car was gone. Most of the lights in the house were off when the cab dropped Rory at 632 Hammock Lane. He said a little prayer of thanks to whatever deity might happen to be listening. It meant he wouldn't have to make idle social chat. He and the O'Mearas had hardly had time to talk after the attack on them this afternoon, what with the light brigade of cops nosing all over the grounds. Rory had claimed he had a date he didn't want to break, and disappeared after a rushed shower and change of clothes.

Inside the house he was surprised not to be greeted by the lingering odors of dinner. Perhaps, after the trauma Sheila suffered, Tom had taken the family out to eat. Eager to miss their return, Rory raced for the basement stairs and descended them two at a time. He made a beeline for the bath, eager to get his hands on the cash before he thought about what he might stuff into his duffel for the long, arduous boat trip.

The instant he flipped the switch to the over-cabinet light he saw the hamper pushed aside. With his access hole to the subbasement revealed, Rory froze. Then he heard a noise behind him, at the far end of the basement, and whirled.

Back lit by the glow of a beer sign, Tom O'Meara sat on a bar stool, an open bottle of Bud Light in one hand and that rucksack full of IRA cash on the oak at his elbow.

"Who the hell are you?" Tom asked, his tone flat.

Rory emerged from the bath, still unable to clearly see O'Meara's face.

"Why did you bring this into my house?" Tom demanded. He touched the rucksack lightly with the bottom of his beer bottle. "After that story you told me last night, I'm thinking guns."

Rory stopped twenty feet from O'Meara, but didn't reply. All he could think of now was Sean in the trunk of that car, bleeding like a stuck pig and terrified out of his wits.

"A man stuck a gun to my wife's head, you son-ofabitch. If we hadn't gotten lucky, our three little girls might be orphans right now."

"Aye, Tom. It's true," Rory admitted. "I'm truly sorry."

"Hot date my ass. Where did you really go when you left here?"

"T' make sure what happened here this afternoon never happens t' y' again."

Tom took a pull off that beer and slammed the bottle down on the bar. "Everything you told us about you is lies, isn't it?"

Devaney shook his head. "Not how I feel about you, Sheila, and the girls, Tom. I swear t' Jaysus, I never meant what came down t'day t' happen. But it did, and now I'm in a bit of a tight spot. I wish I had time t' explain, but I don't. I'll just get my gear and be gone."

"What's the money for, Rory . . . or whatever your name is. It's for guns, right?"

"I need that money right now t' save a man's life, Tom. A man I've fought shoulder t' shoulder wit' since I was fifteen."

O'Meara drained his bottle and threw it clattering into the waste bin behind the bar. "Save him so you can do what? Buy more guns so that more eight-year-old boys can watch their fathers get shot down? In the name of what, Rory?"

Frustrated, Devaney lost his temper. "For fook sake, Tom! If all this were taken from y' today, who would you be?" He waved a hand, gesturing at the house around them. "If you and yours were spat on, told y' were nothing but shit, how would you react?" He shifted from one foot to the other, his eyes back on that knapsack that could buy Sean's life. "I know what it's like because I've lived it, man! I've tried t' make sense of it and I can't. No man with any sense of dignity can."

O'Meara laid a hand on the knapsack, thumb and forefinger toying with the zipper tab. "I let this money leave this house, more people are gonna get killed."

Rory spread his hands to plead his case. "I'm a soldier, Tom. Fighting an ugly, insidious little war that you could never understand. And people get killed in wars. That's true."

The sound of a car pulling up outside drew Devaney's attention. Sheila and the kids, back from a run for burgers or pizza. He glanced in the direction of a closing car door sound. When his gaze returned to O'Meara, he found Tom's service weapon pointed at him.

"I'm placing you under arrest, Rory. I don't see I've got much choice."

Devaney shook his head sadly and sighed. "I'm sorry it had t' end this way between us, Tom. But I can't let y' arrest me. Y've got no idea what awaits me down that road. Y' won't give me the money, fine. But if y' want t' stop me from leavin', you'll have t' shoot me." He turned to start for the stairs.

O'Meara had told Eddie Diaz where to find the door key he'd left outside. As soon as Diaz used it to enter the house, he heard voices in the basement and started that way. From the top of the stairs he caught enough to know he shouldn't descend un-armed. What the hell this was about, he had no idea. Tom and the Irish guy, Rory, were into it about wars, guns, and killing, and he was hearing a hard edge in the Irishman's voice that wasn't there at Morgan's confirmation.

Rory was so intent on watching the sarge, seated over there at his little bar, that he almost walked into the muzzle of Eddie's weapon. When Diaz cleared his throat to warn him off, Devaney nearly jumped out of his shoes. He spun to face Eddie straight on, and Tom timed a leap from his bar stool so perfectly that he had the guy in three quick strides. One moment Rory was registering surprise. The next, O'Meara had him by the wrist to throw a hammer lock and slam him face first into the basement wall. The sarge had cuffs ready for the next move, shook the hasps loose, and quickly snapped both bracelets tight.

19

━━━━━ ◆ ━━━━━

For the first time in his three-year partnership with Sergeant Tom O'Meara, Eddie Diaz's boss had asked him to drive. He'd placed a call to the Operations Desk at One Police Plaza in downtown Manhattan to say they were bringing in a suspected IRA terrorist, and now rode shotgun to keep one eye on Rory Devaney while Diaz got them headed toward the police headquarters building. Because they had neither a radio nor a cellular phone, they were out of communication for the duration of their journey.

For a while, before they crossed the bridge into Brooklyn and started for the Battery Tunnel along the Belt Parkway, Diaz tried to make conversation with the suspect, catching glimpses of his sullen scowl in the rearview mirror. An obstinate Devaney refused to utter so much as a syllable, even when Eddie pressed him for information about this guy whose life he claimed he had to save.

"Gonna probably be some kinda wild clusterfuck downtown, this dude turns out to be the real deal," Eddie told Tom as they finally approached the tunnel. "Everybody from the Feebs to the State Department to the British fucking Embassy is gonna want a piece of this action." He shook his head in amazement. "Two fucking million in cash. Wow. All them cold simoleons sitting there in the trunk give me the heebies, just thinking about them."

O'Meara changed the subject. "Terry Kelly told me today that the D.A. might take your shooting to a grand jury, Eddie."

Diaz glanced sharply at him. "Based on what?" And why, he wondered, had Tom been talking to a brass hat like Kelly in the first place?

"They consider one of those two eyewitnesses to be too reliable. The one who says she saw me pick up the gun," O'Meara replied.

Eddie felt cold sweat break out in his armpits and at the small of his back. "Yeah? And?"

"Because the mutt took two shots at you, he doubts a grand jury will agree to hear it. Still, he wants us both to be prepared for the eventuality."

"Wonderful," Eddie growled. Out the far end of the tunnel, they surfaced into the canyons of the financial district. He caught Church Street going north toward Fulton. At that time of night, this area of the city was like a ghost town. Pleased to finally be behind the wheel, even if he was driving his own car, Diaz wasn't about to disappoint his boss by not making good time. "I seen that look in your eye yesterday, Sarge. After you gave your statement to the shooting panel. Stand-up or not, you hated being put in that spot."

O'Meara quit watching Devaney for a moment to look over at the younger cop. "How you think I'm gonna feel, this does go to the grand jury, Eddie? How can I look some citizen in the eye, and tell them she's a liar?"

Diaz had made the turn from Fulton onto Park Row, drawing them to within two blocks of the headquarters building, when a carting company truck pulled sideways across the road, one block up, and commenced to deliver a thirty-yard Dumpster to a construction site.

"Get a load o' this asshole," Eddie complained. Stopped dead in the street, he was forced to sit impatiently while the trucker climbed out to check his rear clearance. He laid on the horn, and the trucker turned to scowl at him, giving him the finger. That was the trigger. Eddie was out of the car, headed for the driver, his shield case in hand.

"Aw, for crissakes," Rory heard Tom O'Meara moan.

Without appearing to move, he'd taken advantage of the distraction as soon as O'Meara's partner leapt from the car. He'd slouched down and gotten his cuffed hands beneath his buttocks. Now, as Tom leaned further forward in his seat to get a better view of the confrontation, Rory slouched further down to wriggle his cuffed hands forward to a spot just behind his knees. Outside the windshield, Diaz and the trucker were really getting into it, both of them gesticulating wildly with their arms and shouting. Any progress toward delivering that garbage scow onto the sidewalk was stopped dead.

Irritated with his hot-blooded sidekick, Tom ran his window down and hollered to him to back off. Rory used the opportunity to lift both his knees to his chin and pass the handcuff chain beneath his feet. As soon as O'Meara drew his head back into the car, Rory lashed out with the hardened steel bracelets, making impact. Tom grunted and wavered where he sat, dazed. As he seemed to get a handle, and started to react, Rory dropped back onto the seat and lashed out at Tom's bleeding head with one foot. The heel of his sneaker connected with O'Meara's jaw, right on the button. Tom went hard into the dashboard, knocked cold.

Without a second to waste, Rory went over the seat after Eddie Diaz's keys and Tom's gun. His heart beating wildly, pulse pounding at his temples, he sorted through the ring until he found a cuff key. Then he prayed, inserted it into the first bracelet, and turned. It was possible that this was his lucky day after all. The hasp dropped open, his two hands suddenly free.

With one eye on Diaz and the truck driver, Rory slipped from the car and started around it toward the trunk. He'd almost made it when the motion of the closing car door must have caught the Latino cop's attention.

"Hey!" Diaz shouted, and started to run back toward the car. Rory could imagine what he was seeing. O'Meara slouched forward in his seat, head pressed to the windshield with blood pouring from the handcuff blow's nasty gash. From where Diaz stood, it probably looked like his partner was dead.

So far as Rory was concerned, with Sean Geary's life hanging in the balance, he had no choice but to grab that cash locked in the trunk. Diaz would try to stop him unless he did something fast.

Devaney crouched down behind the back of the car and leapt up to level Tom O'Meara's gun at Diaz.

"Stop!" he yelled. "Drop your fookin' gun!"

Rather than comply, Diaz aimed his own weapon and fired. It was hard enough to hit anything with accuracy, firing a handgun standing still. Shooting on the run, Eddie's bullet plowed into the windshield of the car over the steering wheel, two feet low and to the right of his mark. Reflexively, Rory fired back, his first shot taking Diaz mid-chest. A second bullet caught the oncoming cop in the shoulder and spun him like a top.

Suddenly fueled by adrenaline and instinct, Rory fumbled for the trunk key with shaking hands and managed to jam it into the lock. The car shook and he looked up in surprise to see O'Meara, revived, out of his seat and coming at him. Tom was diagonally across the trunk lid from Rory when he suddenly launched into midair. The impact of his flying tackle sent Rory sprawling, but the Irishman managed to hang onto that gun. O'Meara also landed hard, and as Rory scrambled to grab the trunk key again, a bloodied and crazed O'Meara struggled to right himself. In a last-ditch lunge of desperation, he slammed the heel of his hand into Devaney's fingers just as they managed to find the key. A searing bolt of pain shot from Rory's fingers to his elbow, while the shank of the key snapped off in the lock.

He had no options left. Realizing he was done for if he didn't move quickly, Rory surged to his feet to flee. Down the street behind him, a number of other cars blocked by the carting truck had started to honk their horns. As soon as the shooting started, the driver himself had dived for cover and was nowhere to be seen. Others who had seen Diaz go down had also scrambled for cover. Within the short distance of just two blocks, as Rory zigged past the barricades into the park out front of City Hall, he was suddenly the only pedestrian in sight. It took effort, but he forced himself to slow, his heart still pounding furiously and breath coming hard. That handgun tucked out of sight, he ran fingers back through his short blond hair, trying to comb it, straightened his jacket, and continued west toward the Park Place subway stop. It was nine forty-five. He didn't have Burke's money, and he'd very likely just killed a policeman. Perhaps it wasn't his, or Sean's, lucky night after all.

* * *

Ostensibly set up as a stag-night poker party while his wife was away visiting family upstate, the gathering that Megan Desmond could hear downstairs from her room in the Fitzsimmons town house was, in fact, her employer's attempt to insulate himself from any catastrophe that might be headed his way from across the sea. Not a one of the invitees present at that gathering was anything less than a deputy mayor in the current city administration. One was a State senator, down from Albany early for Thanksgiving. Several were titans of Wall Street.

With her plane for Dublin due to leave early the next morning, Megan had waited to hear word from Frankie McGuire all afternoon and evening. The plan, as it stood, was that she complete her mission and return to New York, Sunday next. That was just four days to travel north, make contact with his brigade, and obtain their assurances that all would be ready when he made landfall. All the same, because the situation over there was in a state of flux with the death of Martin McDuff, Rory had told Megan he would contact her, if for no other reason than to wish her Godspeed.

When the phone rang at five minutes past ten, Megan was certain it was Frankie calling for her. When, several minutes later, a knock came at her door, she was not surprised it had taken the judge so long to summon her. He'd shown no interest these past few days in doing anything but distance himself as far from Frankie McGuire as he could.

When she answered her door, Megan was taken aback by the look on Judge Fitzsimmons's face. All the blood was drained from it. She would swear that his hands were shaking, though he tried to hide it by clasping them together.

"Something terrible has happened," he whispered. "Tom O'Meara and his wife were attacked in their home this afternoon. He arrested Frankie, as a suspected IRA terrorist. Somehow, on their way into police headquarters in lower Manhattan, Frankie managed to escape. He killed a policeman in the process."

Megan's hand flew to her mouth. "Oh my God! Where is he now?"

"Good question," Judge Fitz replied. "That was a friend of mine on the city desk at the *Post*. Word is that Frankie got away."

The emergency room at the Beekman-Downtown Hospital was swarming with uniformed and plainclothes police, as well as reporters. Tom O'Meara sat in a bright-lit examining area, getting the large gash from his left eye to chin sewn up with dozens of tiny, delicate stitches. As soon as the ER staff had seen the depth and extent of the cut those handcuffs had inflicted, they'd put out a call for the young plastic surgeon at O'Meara's side. Word had gotten around that Tom's partner was killed in the same fracas that had earned him that gash. When in his presence, the hospital staff spoke in respectful, subdued tones.

A nurse poked her head into the room. "There's a Chief Kelly here to see him, Doctor. Can I show him in?"

"Yes," O'Meara answered for the surgeon. "It's important, Doc."

A moment later, Terry Kelly appeared, dressed in gray worsted pinstripe and an emerald-green tie. He paused at a respectful distance to survey the damage done to his old friend. At least what damage was visible. He met anger and grief in Tom O'Meara's eyes. "I guess asking you how you feel would be a stupid question," he muttered.

Unwilling to disturb the surgeon's delicate work, O'Meara simply closed his eyes slowly, then opened them again.

"There are some people here to see you, Tommy. From the FBI."

Tom felt muscles of his back and neck tighten. Beneath the veneer of happy coooperation that the Justice Department and NYPD brass liked to project, a certain amount of hostility existed between Feeb field agents and the job's rank and file. When the FBI stepped into a case, they often also stepped all over it.

"This houseguest of yours is big, they tell me. Huge, as a matter of fact. They're loaded for bear."

"This is still going to take a while," the surgeon interrupted. "Can they wait?"

"Sorry, Doctor," Kelly apologized. "But I don't think so."

* * *

Only minutes after Judge Fitzsimmons visited Megan Desmond to report on that phone call he'd received, she was startled to hear a light tapping on the window that led to the fire escape. She spun, frightened, and saw Frankie McGuire huddled out there in the cold. The window had a security gate she had to release before she could raise the sash. When she did, Frankie slipped soundlessly into the room, along with a rush of frigid arctic air. Clad only in a thin flannel nightgown, Megan shivered as she eased the sash down again, suddenly self-conscious. She hugged herself as she turned to stare at him.

"The jooge just got a phone call, Frankie. Jaysus and Mary. What happened?"

"Burke's got Seanie," Frankie replied. "And sent people t' Tom and Sheila's t' try and hijack our cash. Tom put two and two together, I'm afraid."

"Jooge Fitz says y' killed a policeman, Frankie."

As tightly wound as a caged panther, Frankie paced quickly back and forth across her tiny, fourth-floor room. "Tom and his partner, Eddie Diaz, were takin' me in, Megan. T' their headquarters buildin' downtown. I couldn't let 'em do that. I'm extradited t' England, I'll be tried and hanged." He stopped his pacing to look directly at her. "Or better yet, shot in transit, while tryin' t' escape."

She thought about the elaborate plan they'd put together over the past several days, and what these developments might mean to them, now. "Y' said Burke's got Sean. What does that mean?"

"I won't find out until I meet wit' him. An hour and a half from now, just a few blocks west o' here. I'm supposed t' bring what money we have, only I don't have it anymore." He lifted his empty hands as he said it and looked down at himself. "Damn, it's hot in here. Y' mind if I take off me coat?"

She told him of course not, and, when he did, took it to throw it across the room's one comfortable chair. Beneath the coat, he had a large revolver stuffed into the waistband of his trousers. "What happened t' the money, Frankie? How can y' buy Burke's missiles without it?"

He started pacing again, though less agitated now. "I need t' worry about Seanie first, Megan. And then the bloody missiles. Burke is expectin' me t' appear with a large bag o' money. I've got to at least make it look like I've brought it. Buy m'self time to see what happens next."

"So you need a duffel," she said, and hurried to her closet. "T' make it look right, we can stuff it with magazines 'n' such."

When Terry Kelly returned to the treatment room he was accompanied by two men in trench coats and off-the-rack suits, and a third in a Burberry raincoat and a suit of tailored gray tweed. "This is Agent-in-Charge Evan Stanley, FBI's Southern District of New York field office. And U.S. Attorney, Art Fisher." Terry introduced the Feds first. "And Harry Sloan, Special Branch of Her Majesty's Secret Service, MI5."

Tom O'Meara's eyes stayed on the third man. His presence in this room meant that Rory Devaney, or whatever his name was, hadn't just leapt from the sea into Tom's net by happenstance. Two million dollars in cash, especially if it was earmarked to buy guns, was big. Which meant Rory was big enough to be entrusted with such responsibility. Tom had seen the real fear in Devaney's eyes when he'd placed him under arrest. It wasn't jail he was afraid of, but something much more ominous. And one look at Harry Sloan told O'Meara he'd just met that nemesis in the flesh.

"Who is Rory Devaney?" he asked, still careful not to move his head. With all that Xylocaine injected into his face, he could feel no more than the occasional remote tug at his flesh, and had to keep reminding himself to stay still.

Agent-in-Charge Stanley stepped across to hand Tom a manila folder. Its contents were scant, but enough for him to get the picture. Or pictures, as it were. The first was of Rory Devaney with much longer hair and a full beard. Grainy in texture, but still good enough to show those intent blue eyes, and the fact that in this shot Rory was perhaps five years younger.

"Your houseguest of the past six weeks is Francis Xavier McGuire, Sergeant. Aka Frankie the Angel. Born twenty-seven of July, 1966. Belfast, Northern Ireland."

As he listened, O'Meara flipped to another photograph. This was a mug shot of a boy no more than fifteen or sixteen, but in his eyes Tom could see that same haunting rage he'd seen so many times as a street cop in the urban ghettos. It was the face of tragedy. A boy becomes a man too soon in time.

"By age eighteen he was unit commander, Falls Road Active Service Unit, Belfast Brigade, Provisional Irish Republican Army," Stanley continued. "Since seventeen, he's been wanted for the crime of murder. A bomb he planted killed three British soldiers. Since then, his body count has risen considerably."

Tom glanced through a series of other photographs, each stamped with the word DECEASED.

"Those three were all members of McGuire's hit team," Stanley explained. "Hunted down for the same crimes for which McGuire and that other man, Sean Geary, are also wanted. The murders of thirteen British Army soliders, eleven Belfast police officers, and an unknown number of civilians."

Hunted down and apparently killed, O'Meara noted. Swift justice was often the rule in times of war, but it wasn't the American way. Not in peacetime. He wondered again about the presence of the MI5 man as he thumbed through pictures of dead soldiers, the wrecked facade of a department store, and a blown-up armored vehicle.

"There's one thing I'm not clear about," the British Special Branch man spoke up. "Just what your relationship to Frankie McGuire is, Sergeant O'Meara."

Tom glanced to Terry Kelly. "What's his capacity here?" he asked.

Agent-in-Charge Stanley answered for the chief. "Our State Department has asked us to cooperate with Mr. Sloan in his investigation, as part of an ongoing liaison effort aimed at combating terrorism on both our shores."

O'Meara half-expected Stanley to sing alternating verses of "My Country 'Tis of Thee," and "God Save the Queen." "What sort of jurisdiction does he have here?" he pressed.

Stanley looked irritated. "I don't think that is quite the issue, Sergeant. He's in pursuit of a mad-dog killer who just shot your partner down in cold blood."

Not quite cold blood, Tom reflected. As much as he mourned the death of Eddie Diaz, he and Eddie had both fucked up, and he knew it. Rory, or Frankie, or whoever the hell he was had taken pains to explain to Tom that he was a soldier, waging war. If Tom had taken the time to weigh what he'd been told more carefully, he might have better understood what Rory's fears were, and taken greater precautions. Rory was a trapped animal, undoubtedly doomed to die if captured. He'd been sent to America on a mission, one important enough to see two million dollars in cash placed in his hands. His arrest meant he'd failed on two fronts. He'd failed to accomplish whatever he'd set out here to do, and he'd forever removed himself from a fight that was clearly his passion. If anyone had any doubt about that, all they needed to do was look at the eyes of the sixteen-year-old boy in that picture. Tom never should have let Eddie jump out of the car. He never should have taken his eyes off Rory, all the way to One Police Plaza. And maybe he shouldn't have arrested the man. It wasn't his and Eddie's war that had cost Diaz his life. It was Harry Sloan's war, and all those dead soldiers and cops in those pictures. All of them had picked up arms to wage it. Some had paid the ultimate price. Big boys' rules. Rory knew what they were, so did Tom, and so did Eddie Diaz.

"I asked what your relationship to Frankie McGuire is," Sloan repeated. There was an edge of impatience in his voice.

"I never knew him by that name," Tom replied. "To me and my family, he was Rory Devaney. A young Irish guy moved here to the States, to try and make a new life for himself."

"And he wound up lodging with you. Why?" Sloan asked. "Just because you and your wife are Irish?"

"So's Cardinal O'Connor," Tom growled. "He ended up with us because we had the room . . . and a friend asked if we would mind."

"What friend?" Sloan pressed.

O'Meara thought about trying to protect Pete Fitzsimmons, and then thought of Sheila, with that sawed-off shotgun jammed up under her chin. He thought of how close he'd come to losing her that afternoon. "A State Supreme Court Judge named Fitzsimmons. When I was a rookie cop, his father was my first commander."

Tom saw Terry Kelly glance curiously at him. Agent Stanley and Harry Sloan exchanged meaningful looks.

U.S. Attorney Art Fisher stepped into the conversation now. "Mr. Sloan has been granted authority by our State and Justice Departments to pursue Francis McGuire with the assistance and full cooperation of the FBI and local law enforcement agencies, Sergeant O'Meara."

Tom tossed the folder onto the examining table at his side. "I thought it interesting to note, Mr. Fisher, that none of those other three fellas on McGuire's team ever quite made it to trial. That make you just a little bit uncomfortable, being sworn as you are to uphold the fifth amendment and all?"

Kelly saw where this might go, knowing how stubborn O'Meara could be once he got his heels dug in. He stepped between his old friend and Fisher. "Don't piss your career away over this, Tommy," he begged. "Cooperate with them. This man McGuire is notorious."

O'Meara stared hard at him. "They'll kill him, Terry." He gestured toward Harry Sloan. "I've been a street cop thirty years. I know that look when I see it in a man's eyes."

20

◆

The black nylon duffel that Megan Desmond dug out of her closet was stuffed full of back issues of fashion magazines and law journals retrieved from a pile in the basement. When Frankie finished fiddling with the zipper, he stood and hefted it. The bulk felt about right.

"Does the jooge have a gun in the house, do y' know?" he asked. He placed the bag on the floor below the fire-escape window, checked the time, and saw he still had an hour and a quarter.

"Two at least, that I know of," she replied. "One in his desk in the li'bry, and one in the chest beside his bed."

Rory liked the long barrel of Tom O'Meara's service weapon for its accuracy, but after the exchange that had killed Eddie Diaz, it only had four bullets left. "Is either of them thirty-eight caliber?"

She nodded. "The one beside his bed. A little short-barreled revolver."

"I need more ammunition, Megan," he told her. "Do y' think you could get it for me?"

She told him to wait where he was, and returned in less than ten minutes with a box of twenty-five hollow point loads. As she watched him fill both pockets of his pants with them, and dump the two spent shells from the cylinder of his weapon to replace them, she moved to the edge of her bed and sat. "I still don't understand what y' hope y' can accomplish, Frankie."

He snapped the cylinder of the gun shut and spun it. "The tug's got three thousand gallons of fuel aboard, and dry and canned provisions enough for a month or more. I'm goin' back t' Belfast, Megan. With or without those missiles. Sean and me."

"So y' still want me t' leave on that plane tomorrow. Set the whole thing up, just as we planned."

He moved to her side and sat with her. "Unless y've heard differently, yes. Tom O'Meara's not likely t' keep how I came t' be in his house a secret. As soon as the cops make that connection, they'll come here t' roust the jooge. You're all packed. Y've got a friend y' could stay wit', until the morning?"

She said she did; a cousin Mary who worked as a barmaid on Broadway, in the Kingsbridge section of the Bronx. She rose from the edge of the bed to find the phone number, scribbled it on a piece of paper, and handed it to McGuire. "If anythin' changes, y'll call me there?"

He reached out to place both his hands on her hips, the warmth of them like a mild shock of electricity through the thin gown. "Wish me luck?" he asked.

She took a step forward to lean into him and take his head in her hands. With no self-consciousness now, she cradled it between her breasts. "We've already got enough martyrs for this bloody fucking cause, Frankie. We don't need another. Do y' understand me?"

He turned his head to nuzzle her, his hands sliding down over her hips and thighs to gather up the hem of the gown. They found the bare flesh of her legs. "We need heroes, not martyrs," he agreed. "You tell them that I'm comin', love. That I intend t' sail that little tug clear across the sea, and straight up those Brit lads' arses."

With her hands still on either side of his head, she eased back to look down into those remarkable, piercing blue eyes. "When I saw it was you on the stairs t' other night, I didn't trust myself t' believe it. Not just then at any rate. I do believe it now, though. Y've got beautiful eyes and beautiful hands, Frankie McGuire."

Slowly, he eased those hands up over her backside, and around across her belly to her breasts. "Kiss me," he growled.

Megan fell forward to topple him back onto the

bed, the fire that had been smoldering in her these past two weeks now suddenly fanned to white heat. Young and strong, she clamped her thighs around his hips and met him hunger for hunger. His meeting with Billy Burke was scheduled for midnight, which meant he needn't leave her side for another hour yet. She meant it to be the longest hour he'd ever spent on earth, and she, too. And so agonizingly delicious, he would remember its taste for an eternity.

Tom O'Meara, left to himself in his treatment room at Beekman-Downtown Emergency, sat angry and dejected on an uncomfortable chair. Those injections of Xylocaine had begun to wear off and the pain of his wound was returning. Reluctant to see his processes dulled, he'd pocketed the pain pills the nurse had handed him, and now tried to distract himself by considering just where he stood. Terry Kelly, the Feds, and the cold-blooded MI5 man had all left to confer together, elsewhere. He had no doubt that any minute now, Pete Fitzsimmons would get a knock at the door. For Pete, it was likely to be a long, profoundly unpleasant night. Not that Tom minded or cared. It seemed clear to him now that his old mentor's boy was thick with the Provisional IRA, that he'd knowingly planted this nightmare in his and his family's lives. Tom hoped to see him in hell for that. As long as he lived, he doubted he would ever be able to shake the vivid memory of Sheila with that gun to her head.

But as much as he hated Pete Fitzsimmons for what he'd done to his family, O'Meara stll couldn't abide by what he saw about to happen. As much as Rory Devaney was a killer in the name of a cause, that MI5 man, Sloan, was a killer who hid within the sanctuary of government. There was only one way that Devaney should be made to answer for his crimes. If hunted and captured on American soil, he was subject to the laws that O'Meara swore thirty years ago to defend. They granted any man the right to due process. Despite the mistake he made on the street two days ago, Eddie Diaz died believing that. Tom would die believing it, too.

O'Meara was tired of sitting there feeling sorry for himself. Suddenly, he was on his feet and grabbing for his jacket. The plainclothes and uniformed cops still loitering with reporters in the waiting area were so preoccupied, only a handful even looked up to notice the man with his head shrouded in a towel hurrying past. On the street, luck was with him. A drunk who had fallen and struck his head in a bar near the South Street Seaport was being helped by two friends from a cab.

Judge Pete Fitzsimmons, aware of how slowly the wheels of justice often turned, was surprised when his doorbell rang so soon. He'd received that call from the city desk man at the *Post* a little over an hour ago. Judge Pete had played some excellent poker that night, in spite of being preoccupied. He hated to lay down the Queen-high straight he held to answer the door.

Fitzsimmons could imagine the look of shock on his own face, when he saw Tom O'Meara's face was swathed in bandages. Hatless, Tom looked too hot under the collar to appear even remotely uncomfortable in weather ten degrees below freezing.

"Tom!" the judge greeted him. "I just now heard what happened to you tonight. I'm so sorry about Eddie. He was a good man."

"Cut the crap, Pete," O'Meara snapped. He stepped up to push past the judge without invitation, and stood there in the entry hall listening to the laughter and joking in the card room, three doors along. "You and me are gonna talk. Now."

Always a master at turning on a dime, no matter what corner he found himself in, Pete threw the wheel over hard, steering for safer ground. "I had no idea who the kid was, Tommy. On that, I swear to God Almighty. My cousin Patrick called, said he had a boy needed a leg up. You know how I've helped other kids like him before."

Rather than bite, O'Meara reached out, grabbed him by his tie, and slammed him hard into the wall behind. Before Pete could recover from the shock of it, Tom slapped him across the face. "There's a man from Britain's Special Branch here, working with the FBI to hunt him down," he snarled. "There's no doubt in my mind, he finds him before I do, he's gonna shoot him like a rabid dog. Before he does that, he'll come here and crawl up your ass."

Part of Pete Fitzsimmons wanted to get outraged. That was the sancrosanct, State Supreme Court Justice part of him. He'd never been slapped in the face in his adult life. But this was a thirty-year cop confronting him, a man who dealt day in and out with real bad guys. Everything about him said he meant business, and knew how to conduct it to his satisfaction. Pete looked nervously toward the open card room door, then motioned O'Meara up the stairs toward his second-floor library.

Once the door was closed to seal them in the privacy of his book-lined refuge, Fitzsimmons sighed. "Okay. Exactly what is it you need to know?"

"What's the money for?" O'Meara asked. "What in the name of Christ did he plan to buy with two million dollars?"

If any color remained in Pete's face, he knew it must have drained away, too. "How do you know about the money?"

Tom took a surprisingly quick step toward him, fist raised to strike him again. "Any second now, I'm gonna start breaking body parts, Pete. I swear to Christ."

Their naked bodies entwined in the aftermath of lovemaking, the sweat of their exertion drying cool across his exposed shoulders and back, Frankie felt Megan tense in his arms at the faint sound of the doorbell, downstairs. He knew it wasn't wise for him to have stayed here as long as he had, and as reluctant as his heart was, he started to disengage himself.

"Tom O'Meara has surely told them of my connection t' Jooge Pete by this time," he whispered. "It won't be that long before his Irish nanny is dragged into it, too. We should away, love. Quickly."

"The man's name is Burke," Pete Fitzsimmons told O'Meara. This was abject surrender. He was a traitor to a cause that his dead father had once held as dear to his heart as the flag of these United States. But O'Meara was right. If a British agent managed to get his hands on the likes of Frankie McGuire here in America, the likelihood of him making it to a London courtroom was a very small one, indeed. And all because Billy Burke, a fair-weather friend if ever the IRA had one, had decided to take advantage of a turn in Provo fortunes. "He's got a string of bars through Hell's Kitchen. The one he uses for his base of operations is on the corner of Ninth and Forty-fourth. He's an old Westie, and a weapons merchant."

"So Devaney is here to buy guns."

Fitzsimmons shook his head. "Stinger missiles. Burke has a line on a shipment, smuggled out of Afghanistan."

Tom stared at Fitzsimmons in disbelief. "Those things can take down an airliner, Pete."

"Or a British Army helicopter gunship. The commanders of the Belfast Brigade are desperate to even the playing field again."

"Some game," O'Meara muttered in disgust.

"The woman who works as our nanny has been

McGuire's contact these past two weeks," Fitzsimmons told him. "She talked to him this afternoon. Burke has taken another Falls Road Unit soldier hostage. A friend of McGuire's named Geary. When Frankie produces the money, he gets both Geary and the missiles."

"When?" Tom demanded.

"Midnight, she said. Somewhere on Greenwich Street, in the meatpacking district."

"And after that, he takes the missiles where?"

"To load them aboard the tug he and Geary have spent the past six weeks making seaworthy. It's tied up at a pier off Amboy Road, just a couple miles south of you and Sheila." There was at least a mile of old piers along the Tottenville waterfront. Fitzsimmons believed that if McGuire got that far, he might still have a chance.

"He doesn't have the money anymore, Pete. We do."

Fitzsimmons felt himself blink. "Then it's my guess, a half hour from now, both he and Sean Geary are dead. Burke plays hardball, Tommy."

"The nanny." Tom demanded. "She here now?"

Fitzsimmons considered what he was doing, and wondered how he would be able to live with himself after this. "I expect. Her room is on the fourth floor."

O'Meara grabbed him by the sleeve of his jacket and jerked him toward the library door. "Show me."

* * *

Megan Desmond saw no reason to waste time pulling the window closed behind her as she handed her one suitcase out to Frankie, then climbed out onto the fire escape after it. It was only eleven-thirty and he still had plenty of time to hike those four blocks west to the meatpacking district. Still, he was in a hurry now. The sooner he got to the meeting place, the more time he would have to survey the site and figure out his options.

Once Rory handed Megan from the fire escape ladder to the back-garden pavement, she started toward the basement side door with her key.

"Y've got the money I gave y'?" he asked.

"Aye. And another thousand dollars I've saved from my work here. D' y' want some of it, Frankie?"

As she unlocked the door she heard him grunt. "Where would I spend it, Megan, love? This time tomorrow, I'm either two hundred miles out to sea, or the latest parched throat in hell. There's nothing in the lore says the Devil takes cash. Not e'en from one of his own."

It took Tom O'Meara only an instant, seeing the nanny's open window, to understand what had happened, and how recently. As cold as it was outside, the temperature in that tiny cell of a room wasn't ten degrees cooler than the rest of the house.

"What kind of car does this Burke drive?" he demanded of Fitzsimmons.

"Lexus sedan. Sort of a British racing green," the judge replied.

How appropriate, Tom thought. "Where's your car, Pete?"

"Downstairs on the street. You need a lift somewhere?"

Tom got them started back toward the library. "I need the keys."

When Pete pulled up to protest, O'Meara gave a a none-too-gentle prod.

"And a gun while you're at it. Big, bad IRA sympathizer like you must have a whole fucking arsenal."

21

◆

As vague as the address of the meeting place was—near Horatio, on Greenwich Street—Frankie McGuire had no trouble identifying the location. In an area busy with the hum of commerce, even at that late an hour, the dark green Lexus sedan in which he'd taken his memorable ride that evening stuck out like a boil on a nun's nose. Parked in among the dozens of large and small refrigerated delivery trucks lining the street, it faced a roll-up loading door left three feet open from the pavement. So much for him getting here early enough to survey the lay of things. Whatever reception Burke and his crew had planned for him was already in place.

As Frankie ducked beneath the warehouse door, a half-dozen bare bulbs, suspended on conduit with enameled tin shades, were all that illuminated the gloomy interior. He straightened slowly, the duffel in his left hand, to see both Burke and the goon, Teddy, standing before the open back doors of the same panel van driven to their meet at Jones Beach. The chill air of the place had the heavy stink of dead meat.

"Greetings, Mr. McGuire," Burke's voice boomed out. "You're a few minutes early, I see."

Frankie took a step further into the warehouse and paused to scan the catwalk running overhead along the left wall, from a staircase to a glassed-in office of some sort. Empty, it seemed.

"I hope it's of no great inconvenience t' y', Billy. I've always liked t' be prompt."

Frankie turned to scan into the gloom on the right side of the warehouse, only to have a car's head-lights momentarily blind him as they hit him in the eyes. His free hand came up to shield his vision from the sudden glare as something cold and hard touched the back of his head. He froze.

"Just a formality, Mr. McGuire," Burke's voice echoed through the room again. "In the interest of my peace of mind."

A rough hand pawed over Frankie until it found the revolver in his waistband. Removed, he heard it clatter to the floor before that hand shoved him onward. Overhead on the catwalk, a previously unseen gunman stepped into view from deep shadow.

"Money for missiles," Burke said as he reached to pat one of a dozen crates in the open cargo area of the panel van. "Straight up and simple."

"Badabing, badabing, badaboom, Mr. Burke? I can't believe y've forgotten about Sean." Twelve crates containing three Stingers each brought the total to thirty-six, not sixty.

Billy snapped his fingers and waved to the man who had frisked Frankie. "Of course. Get Geary for Mr. McGuire, Phil. A deal's a deal."

The other henchman hurried toward the parked car with the glaring headlights, popped the trunk, and reached in to grab something. When he emerged back into the light, Frankie saw he carried what looked like a blood-soaked pillow slip. Without a word, he stopped five feet from Frankie and upended the sack to dump Sean's severed head at his feet.

His knees gone weak, McGuire gagged as he stumbled a step backward, fighting to maintain his balance. "Y' fooking bastard!" he snarled at Burke.

Impassive, Billy Burke shrugged. "You want to leave here with these missiles, I think it's time we saw your money, McGuire. It's still nothing but a rumor, until I see the green."

His rage now focused to a dangerously sharp edge, Frankie took three quick strides forward, directly over his dead friend's desecrated head, to place that duffel on the floor between him and Burke. "I'll see y' in hell for this, Billy. Y've my sworn oath on it."

Burke grunted. "Who do you think you're threatening, you bog Irish hick? Look around you. Where's your Irish Republican Army now?" He gestured to Teddy to go get the cash. "When I first learned that you were the famous Frankie McGuire, you couldn't imagine my disappointment."

Teddy advanced to kneel before the duffel and place his machine pistol on the concrete at his side. When he tugged the zipper tab, the striker from a box of wooden kitchen matches, Crazy-Glued to its back, ignited the first of several hundred match heads, all stuffed into a plastic prescription bottle. Startled by the sudden flash of all that phosphorus gone up at once to burn white hot, he reared back just as the compressed butane in a pair of cheap cigarette lighters exploded. In an instant, the resultant fireball engulfed him.

Frankie timed it so that the moment Teddy grabbed that zipper tab, he was poised to launch. The incendiary device was rigged to explode upward, using the floor as a reflector, and Rory went in underneath it, diving to grab the goon's machine pistol just before he tucked his head. Thus protected from flames, Frankie did a swift and graceful somersault. At the other end of it, he righted himself on one knee, his other foot out before him for balance, and sprayed the catwalk overhead with a quick burst from Teddy's weapon. The gunman up there staggered, crashed into the iron pipe railing at his hip, and fell fifteen feet to the floor.

Out of the corner of his eye, McGuire saw Burke run at a crouch toward that parked car. Frankie turned his attention on the man who had frisked him. That man had now recovered from the shock of seeing Teddy go up in flames. He brought the sawed-off shotgun he carried inside his coat into play, and Frankie dove flat on his belly to roll hard as the twelve-gauge roared. Then, before the man could locate him and take aim again, the machine pistol jumped in McGuire's hands. The target danced spasmodically like a marionette manipulated by a maniac, then slammed into the warehouse wall, and collapsed.

Inside that parked car, Billy Burke took aim at Frankie out the windshield and fired twice at him through the glass. McGuire felt the heat of one slug scorch his cheek as it ricocheted off the concrete dangerously close. Still, he didn't flinch or lose focus. Instead, he sighted in on a spot directly between the two holes those shots had created in the windshield. For a moment after he fired, he saw nothing move. Then the passenger door flew open and Burke tried to dive clear, one hand pressed to a spot high on his chest near his shoulder. When he stumbled and fell, Frankie took aim and fired again. This time he hit the scurrying man in the hip.

All was deathly quiet inside the warehouse as McGuire rose to his feet on shaky knees and advanced on the spot where Billy Burke lay bleeding from his wounds.

"Bog Irish hick, indeed," he said, and clucked his tongue as he stared down at his nemesis.

Burke stared back up at him, his breath coming labored. There was something akin to panic in his eyes, tinged perhaps by a bit of surprise.

"When y' see the Devil, tell him I said hello,"
Frankie told him. He flipped the switch on Teddy's
weapon from full auto to single shot, took aim, and
put one bullet in the middle of Billy Burke's forehead. Big boys' rules.

From Pete Fitzsimmons's town house on Tenth
Street near Fifth Avenue, Tom O'Meara drove the
judge's new Lincoln west across Ninth Street to
Christopher and then Greenwich. After thirty years
on the police force, he knew he should have a better
handle on how these streets of old Manhattan, below
Fourteenth Street, ran. But all his life, the West Village had never ceased to confuse him. The meatpacking area was just east of the Hudson River and
south of Fourteenth, but the area he drove through
now, after turning north on Greenwich Street, was
still mostly residential. He scanned street names as
he went, unsure of where Horatio should be. Perry,
West Eleventh, Bank, Bethune, West Twelfth. Any
order between numbered and name streets had no
rhyme nor reason through here, where many buildings dated from before the Revolutionary War, and
few were built later than the turn of the twentieth
century.

As he drove, Tom thought of Pete Fitzsimmons
and the fate most likely in store for his old commander's son. Any minute now, Uncle Sam was
going to come down on him with both feet. By the
time the stomping stopped, Pete would at the very
least be removed from the bench and disbarred. It

was likely he would face felony charges of being an accessory to murder, aiding a fugitive in flight, and perhaps even sedition. No matter how many of those charges stuck, his life, as he knew it, would be ruined.

He passed Jane Street and saw the sign for Horatio. It was the street that appeared to demark the dividing line between a relatively quiet residential area and a chaos of trucks parked every which way. Men in white coats and hard hats loaded and unloaded the trucks. Lights blazed inside cold storage warehouses hung with row upon row of butchered animal carcasses. Tom proceeded slowly up that stretch of Greenwich between Horatio and Gansevoort Streets until a green Lexus sedan blocked his path.

A group of four men in white coats and a truck driver were all in the street around the car, peering in its windows and tugging at the handles of its locked doors. From what O'Meara could see as he pulled over to park, the front end of the car was badly crushed, and the left front fender was scraped as though sideswiped. As he emerged to approach on foot, he noticed skid marks created by the tires. It looked like the parked car most likely had been pushed from in front of a loading door across the sidewalk. A green Lexus. British racing green.

Rather than stop and talk to the men trying to move the car from the road, Tom hurried to that loading door, grabbed one of the handles and heaved to see if he could budge it. Not locked, it rolled upward with such ease that he nearly lost his balance. Beyond, he found a strangely lit warehouse interior. Someone had left a car parked inside with its headlights on. Directly in the path of those beams lay a human corpse burned beyond recognition, and a severed human head. Further back in the empty interior lay two more bodies, one facedown, and one sprawled on his back. The stink of burnt flesh, mixed with the sight of that head on the floor and an underlying slaughterhouse stench, saw O'Meara grab for his nose and mouth. He backpedaled quickly for the street. Tom recognized the face from a photograph seen in Agent-in-Charge Evan Stanley's file folder. That head belonged to Rory's friend, Sean Geary.

As daunting as the notion of sailing a sixty-foot tug across three thousand miles of open Atlantic might be, Frankie McGuire knew he had to blank his mind to all fear. As he took the exit off the Richmond Parkway before the toll booth for the Outerbridge Crossing, and started west on Bridge Street toward Arthur Kill Road, he considered how unlikely it was that he'd gotten this far. Maybe anything *was* possible. No question, two men attempting this feat was a barmy enough notion. One trying it was insanity. But Frankie was now convinced he was crazy to the marrow. Who but a crazy man would have come here believing he could pull this mission off? Yet here he drove toward his boat, in a van loaded with thirty-six gunship killing Stinger missiles, now in Provisional IRA possession.

Deep inside, his heart ached for Sean Geary. He'd loved the man, hyper, woman-chasing, dangerously volatile rogue that he was. He would miss him on this journey, no matter whether he reached Portrush or not. Sean had fought by his side, plotted late into a thousand nights with him, and ultimately laid down his life for their cause. Like Megan's brother, Dessie, and hundreds others, he'd now entered the sacred pantheon of Irish martyrs. For all his reckless shortcomings in life, no one could take that solemn distinction from him in death. On this night, Sean Geary had become an Irish saint.

Frankie found the *Voyager* lying quietly to, moored at a battered old dock alongside the scene of her recent rebirth. At that late hour, the old man in the security shack was half asleep. Frankie drew alongside in the panel van and honked. With a half-fogged nod of recognition, the guard pushed a button on his panel to start the gate open, then stuck his head out into the cold.

"How long y' gonna be?" he hollered.

"Don't worry about me," Frankie replied. "I'm takin' her out early. Gonna sleep aboard."

Each of those twelve missile crates weighed in excess of a hundred pounds. As Frankie rolled down the access road to the dock, he scanned the area for some kind of lift truck or cart. What he spotted wasn't ideal, but would do. A rusty old Radio Flyer wagon, probably abandoned by a former dock tenant and once used to shuttle beer and groceries. He parked the van and retrieved the wagon to begin his unloading, moving quickly now. Down here on the water, the damp mixed with the bitter cold to seep deep toward his bones.

The first crate he dragged aboard was shoved down into the cramped little cordage hold, forward. Then Frankie took a moment to enter the wheelhouse, start the onboard generator to get some heat going, and kicked over the big twelve-cylinder diesel. As the power plant coughed, sputtered, and then clattered to life, he thought again of Sean, and those endless hours of love he'd poured into it.

"Godspeed t' y', friend," he murmured. He said another prayer that all that work had been enough. He'd learned a few things about diesel power from Geary, but nowhere near what it might take to save himself, should that motor quit on him in a twenty-foot storm swell.

It frankly amazed Tom O'Meara that the man he knew as Rory Devaney had been able to get as far that night as he had, considering the circumstances. Three and a half hours ago, Rory was riding handcuffed and unarmed in the custody of two veteran New York police officers. He'd escaped with four rounds of ammunition left after firing two shots from Tom's captured service weapon. What Tom had witnessed inside that warehouse was testament to how he had managed to survive all these years. Most men would fold up their emotional tents if the severed head of a close friend were tossed at their feet. But this guy had responded in a manner that had clearly taken all of his unsuspecting adversaries by deadly surprise. Tom thought he'd seen it all in his thirty years of police service, but he'd never seen anything like what he saw tonight. He tried to imagine how one man with four bullets in his gun could get the drop on three who knew full well to expect him. O'Meara doubted Devaney had ambushed them, because then the guy burned to a crispy critter made no sense. No, Rory had done it from the inside. He'd walked right into the midst of them, two million short of the sum needed to make his deal. He'd been shown the head of his friend, and somehow he'd driven away with the goods.

From Manhattan, Tom drove straight through Brooklyn to the Verrazano-Narrows Bridge and on to Tottenville. It was after one o'clock by the time he arrived at Tottenville Station, the terminus of the Staten Island Rapid Transit Railway. From there, he had two directions he could go in conducting his search. South of him, the old piers and boatyards ran along the Arthur Kill shoreline for less than half a mile before they ended at Amboy Road. Because it would probably be as easy to cover that stretch on foot as it was to drive it, Tom opted to go north up the Ellis Street waterfront, first.

Three times during his run up Ellis, with the span of the Outerbridge Crossing looming across the water in the near distance, he climbed from the cozy warmth of the Lincoln to take a closer look at a tug. In that Polaroid he'd found of Rory, with the pretty woman in his arms, there'd been a carved wooden sign, mounted to the bulkhead behind him. The engraved letters were painted bright white, and spelled out one word. *VOYAGER*. O'Meara knew he was taking a gamble, but wondered how big and what he had to lose, as he searched the stern transom of each vessel for that name.

Improperly named or not, none of the three tugs he encountered at the docks along Ellis Street had a single light burning aboard. No trucks that could convey a load of contraband military hardware were parked in their vicinities. With the clock working against him, Tom abandoned his search of that stretch of waterfront, once Ellis intersected with Arthur Kill Road. He turned right onto the larger artery and ran the mile back south to where it eventually dead-ended. From there he climbed from the car, turned up his collar and started along that last quarter mile of dock area on foot.

The guard in the boatyard security shack looked like he might have been asleep when O'Meara roused him.

"Whadizzit?" he demanded, clearly irritated by the interruption.

Tom showed him his sergeant's tin and ID. "Sergeant O'Meara," he introduced himself. "Mind if I come in? I'm freezing my ass."

It was never hard for any veteran cop to spot another soul who'd shared his burden. The old guy in the pathetic security guard's uniform was NYPD retired, no doubt in O'Meara's mind. Out here by himself in the middle of the night, as far away from the action as a citizen of New York could get without taking a swim. Tom's sympathies went out to him, not the least of them being the knowledge that he would put in his own papers later that morning. Was this what the future had in store?

"What can I do for youse, Sarge? I was twenty-seven years on the job, myself. Until the old lady put the screws on me t' retire and move to Orlando. Six years later, when she drops dead, I got mahjong up the ass and sunshine turnin' my skin to a nuclear waste dump. Back five years now, and I never been happier."

"I hear you," O'Meara replied. "This is probably just a wild-goose chase, but I'm looking for two Irish guys, been working on an old tug around here somewhere. One of them left a wallet full of credit cards on a bar up in New Dorp. Couple patrons said they thought he was headed this way."

"That'd be the *Voyager*." The guard peered out of a window of the shack toward the waterfront as he said it. "And they were right about him comin' here. That's the van he drove up in, half an hour or so ago. Said he had an early run t' make. Thought he'd spend the night. I ain't seen the other one. Sean. Real character, that fella. Got a knack with engines, everyone around here says."

Had a real knack, Tom thought.

22

That hour he'd spent with Megan Desmond was almost as much on Frankie McGuire's mind as was the death of Sean Geary. She was scheduled to depart Newark International for a flight to Dublin's Shannon Airport at ten A.M., which meant departing her friend Mary's house in the Bronx in just six hours. She undoubtedly needed her sleep, but once Frankie slipped his moorings, he would have no means of communicating with anyone in the outside world until he reached landfall. She would want to know he'd been successful, and that her own efforts were more vitally important now than ever. Besides, one more time before he embarked on this perilous journey across the vast, empty sea, he wanted to hear the music of her voice again.

The missiles were loaded securely in the cordage

hold, the diesel was as warm as it would get, as was the wheelhouse, now all snug and cozy. Frankie put a kettle to boil on the galley stove to make tea, ran one last check of his gauges, and hurried out onto the dock to slip all but the two main mooring hawsers. There was a coin phone in the shelter of an equipment shed near the main gate. With the number Megan had given him stuffed in his pants pocket, Frankie started to jog up the dock for his last walk for a long while on dry land.

The car parked at the gate outside the guard shack looked familiar to him, but at first he couldn't figure why. Then it hit him. Judge Pete Fitzsimmons's Lincoln Town Car carried those special license plates of a State Supreme Court Justice. Unable to figure what Judge Fitzsimmons might be doing here, McGuire froze. There was heat sure to come down on the man, now that Tom O'Meara knew who had been planted to live with him and his unsuspecting family. So what had the old fool done? Panicked and come running here in hopes that Frankie might agree to take him back to Northern Ireland?

Torn between his desire to hear Megan's voice, to tell her he was safely away, and the desire to avoid any confrontation with the judge at all costs, Frankie stood in the middle of the boatyard access road. Reluctantly, he realized he could waste no more time here, and started to turn back for the boat. Then the door to the guard shack opened. Instead of Judge Fitzsimmons, it was Tom O'Meara who stepped out into the night and stood staring straight at him. The animal survivor in Frankie knew he couldn't waste time gaping in disbelief. It put spurs to him. He turned and ran.

Tom O'Meara wondered if it was that lingering vision of the severed head on the warehouse floor that prevented him from drawing the 9-mm Beretta automatic Pete Fitzsimmons had provided, and opening fire. Or maybe it was the memory of Eddie Diaz, chasing that unwitting radio thief down Nagle Avenue and shooting him in the back. Either way, or neither, he left the gun stuffed into his waistband, having seen no evidence of Rory being armed. Instead he gave chase.

Within twenty yards of commencing his run down that rutted gravel boatyard road, the old football injury started to scream. Twenty years younger, forty pounds lighter, and without a gate to contend with, Rory had gotten a good jump on him. By the time Tom rounded a bend in the road toward the boat docks, still fifty yards distant, Rory was already aboard his vessel and slipping a first hawser from its dockside bit. Tom ran at him as Rory ran aft, the bow of the boat already starting to drift with the tide into the Arthur Kill channel. Forced to stop and pull slack into the stern mooring line by heaving against it with all his strength, Devaney lost ground to O'Meara before he finally got the line loose enough to flip it free. Then, completely adrift now, he ran for the wheelhouse to grab the helm as Tom's feet finally found the first planks of the dock.

O'Meara was still ten feet from the boat, the night air burning his lungs almost as fiercely as the old injury burned his knee, when the tug's powerful diesel engine suddenly snarled. One moment the vessel was adrift, then its big single screw dug hard to churn the water in its wake to froth. The craft froze in its backward movement, shuddered like a dog shaking water from its coat, and then started to swing quickly around toward the channel. Still running at full tilt, Tom saw any chance of catching his quarry sailing quickly out of reach and abandoned all caution. As the aft port gunwale swept past in its turn, just eight feet from the edge of the dock, Tom planted his good left foot and launched.

While in midair over the cold, frothy waters of Arthur Kill, O'Meara was sure he'd mistimed his jump by much worse than a split second; that he was headed for a drubbing. Then, as if in slow motion, the stern deck of the boat approached achingly closer. Before he could quite ready himself for it, despite all the time it seemed like he'd had, he and it impacted. Hard. The bad knee buckled with a sickening sideways twist and he landed on his right side. The gun wedged into his waistband clattered loose. With mind-numbing pain in his leg, he forced himself to grab for the loose weapon. Up ahead of him, in the dim light of the wheelhouse, he saw Rory peer out into the night to try and catch a glimpse of him. Tom was low to the deck, and wore clothes that made him all but invisible in those conditions. He watched as Devaney, apparently satisfied of his success, poured on yet more power and made for the open water of Raritan Bay.

The lights of the Verrazano-Narrows Bridge were off to the north, and with the glow of Brooklyn and Long Island to guide him eastward, Frankie McGuire now had nothing out front of his rising and plunging bow but open Atlantic. Settled down at the *Voyager*'s helm, his pulse still pounding in his ears, he forced himself to take a deep breath and exhale. Without a doubt, as soon as Tom O'Meara could get to a telephone, he would call out the Coast Guard and perhaps the Pentagon for all Frankie knew. But a sixty-foot boat, well away from land and out to sea, was as easy to locate as a needle in a haystack. With the three thousand gallons of fuel that he and Sean had put aboard, he knew he had enough in reserve to warrant burning a bit extra now. What he needed more than anything was distance, and distance meant speed. Running without lights until daybreak, almost six hours away, he could be at least seventy miles offshore before he would be visible to an air search. Then, if an aircraft did happen to get lucky and spot him, he had a whole forward hold full of Stinger missiles at his disposal.

When the starboard deck hatch flew open and Tom O'Meara appeared from out of the night, an automatic pistol aimed at the center of Frankie's chest, the shock was so profound that McGuire's hands froze on the helm.

"Keep 'em there where I can see them," O'Meara

growled. He slowly advanced into the cabin, noticeably favoring his right leg and wincing with each step.

"Looks like y' hurt yourself jumpin', Tom," Frankie commented.

"Shut up!" O'Meara snarled. His eyes never leaving his quarry's, he eased himself around to where he had a good vantage of the entire bridge area. Carefully, he propped himself against the edge of the chart table for support.

"I'm not goin' back, Tom," McGuire told him. "Either y' let me put y' ashore, or y' kill me."

"Turn this fucking thing around! Now!"

Frankie lifted his hands from the wheel to shrug. "Like I said. I can't, Tom. I'm sorry about your friend, Eddie. Truly I am. But I'm a soldier on a mission. If y'd turned me in, I'd never've made it t' Britain alive."

The gun he'd taken off Tom earlier that night was wedged out of sight beneath his bulky Aran sweater. He didn't want to kill O'Meara, make Sheila a widow and those three sweet girls fatherless, but he'd gotten this far for one reason alone. To go all the way. Even if O'Meara managed to get one bullet into him, he believed he was quick and accurate enough to give back what he got. Unless it was a head or a heart shot, and he doubted it would be either. Tom O'Meara didn't want to kill him.

"The killing's got to stop somewhere, Rory," O'Meara said.

"It's Frankie, Tom. Francis Xavier McGuire. And

you'll have t' kill me t' stop it." He watched
O'Meara's reflection in the windscreen glass. Stale-
mate. "Gets a bit complicated, doesn't it? Y' don't
want t' kill me, and I don't want t' kill you. Let me
put y' ashore up the coast a bit, Tom. Y' can go
home t' your lovely family, and I can try t' do what
I've sworn I will."

"Not a chance," Tom murmured. "You left one
thing out of your equation, friend. You forgot I'm a
cop."

That pain in his knee was burning so bad, O'Meara
could hardly see straight. He wanted Rory, or
Frankie, or whoever the hell he was to just give it
up, turn this damned boat around and head them
toward the NYPD Harbor Unit Charlie pier at the
foot of Fifty-second Street and First Avenue in
Brooklyn. But this wasn't some ordinary bad guy.
This one was a zealot. He had the gleam of Arma-
geddon in his eye.

When Devaney suddenly feinted to his left, then
dove right for the open wheelhouse hatch, Tom shot
to maim, not to kill. His bullet took his target in the
left thigh, slamming him into the edge of the hatch-
way as his momentum took him out onto the deck.
As much as his right knee hated the idea, O'Meara
lurched away from the chart table in pursuit.

On deck, with the tug crashing undaunted through
the windswept chop, O'Meara saw a spatter of blood
smeared off toward the stern deck. He started
around the wheelhouse in the opposite direction.

Crouched low, he was creeping past one of the wheelhouse ports when its glass exploded just inches from his face. Realizing where he must be going, Rory had fired clear through the cabin of the boat, from port to starboard.

"I don't want t' kill y', Tom!" Devaney called out. "I swear t' Jaysus I don't. Please don't make me do it, man!"

In the shifting wind, it was impossible to tell where that voice was coming from. Just to O'Meara's right, he saw a ladder running up the side of the wheelhouse to its roof. He grabbed hold of the rail to head for high ground, his burning knee making progress agonizing, and his head swimming by the time he finally gained his objective. Breathing hard, he lay there flat on his belly and listened hard to the sounds of a boat at sea. The snarling growl of the diesel. The crash of the bow against the chop. The slight, faint clank of metal on metal, and a grunt. Off to his left. There was another ladder on the other side of the wheelhouse, and a wounded Rory Devaney was trying to go for the high ground, too.

With his weapon laid across the spray-dampened surface before him, O'Meara's eyes rapidly adjusted to the gloom. He waited. There was another gasping grunt and faint clunk, and then the top of Rory's blond head appeared in his sights. In memory, another vivid flash of Sheila with that sawed-off shotgun jammed beneath her chin, and the look of absolute terror Tom had seen in her eyes, helped steel him.

Devaney registered surprise as he mounted the next step toward his objective to see the muzzle of O'Meara's gun aimed at him. His shoulder dropped slightly as he shifted to bring his own weapon into play.

"Big boys' rules, remember?" Tom growled, and shot him between the eyes.

EPILOGUE

$\blacklozenge$

Judge Pete Fitzsimmons had returned to the card game in his parlor to play several more hands for appearance' sake. Then he'd excused himself to return back upstairs. Everyone was having such a good time. Pete's excellent whisky was flowing in ample supply and the conversation was so lively, that no one seemed to mind his earlier absence. He doubted they would much mind the second, either.

He sat in his desk chair in his library, framed photographs of his dear departed father, his wife, Juliet, and little Molly all arranged on the blotter before him, and wondered what was taking the FBI, federal attorney, and that British Special Branch fellow so long to get there. Not that it mattered, really. When they did arrive, they would find a coward, dead of his own hand. That is, if Pete could marshall the courage.

He stared at the face of his dead father, and reached to turn those photographs of Juliet and Molly facedown. Neither of them should have to see this, but his father surely deserved no less. It was his father's war he'd tried all his adult life to believe in, and to fight. But here in America, raised with all her creature comforts, he'd never been able to find the fire in his belly and ice in his heart that two years in a prison ship had bestowed upon his uncles.

"I tried, Pop," he murmured. And as he lifted that snub-nosed revolver, carried here from the nightstand beside his bed, he felt his hands start to shake. He wept. Somewhere on the south tip of Staten Island, Frankie McGuire was either making his run toward a revolutionary hero's welcome home, or Tommy O'Meara had hunted him down and stopped him. If O'Meara failed, did it really matter a whit, he wondered? How could missiles help end eight hundred years of hatred?

With the gun cradled in his big, meaty paws, he heard the doorbell downstairs. A moment later, voices raised in animated conversation reached the library, and then the sound of footfalls on the stairs. Pete wiped his eyes with the back of one hand and sighed.

He faced his father and muttered in disgust, "Ah, well."

The gun stuffed between his teeth, he bit hard on the barrel and pulled the trigger.